CONTENTS

KT-363-914

LUDEC

THE BATTLE OF HASTINGS 1067

STEPHEN ATKINSON

Published by
Eleusinian Press Ltd
www.eleusinianpress.co.uk

Printed and bound in Great Britain by
Copytech design

A catalogue record for this book
is available from The British Library

ISBN 978-1-909434-11-4

CHAPTER ONE
A VICTORY SOURED

September, 1066. Stamford Bridge: A Victory Soured

Three runaway farm boys stand drenched in the rain on the edge of a muddy track. One has a short sword, old and rusted, the second a pitchfork and the third a pair of ugly hammers stuck in his belt.

"For England! For the King!" the tallest one yells, but his voice is lost in the ceaseless heavy drizzle and the overpowering roar of this massive army on the move. The soldiers don't notice them, all eyes clamped on the cloying mud at their feet.

This is Harold's army returning triumphant from the north, Viking blood still glistening red on sword and shield, now marching south to meet the Norman invaders on the beaches of Sussex.

They are largely a rag-tag, motley bunch of farmers, more eager to get home to their fields than to take up arms against a foreign foe, however pressing the need. Apart from the King's own Housecarls they are undertrained and poorly armed, often wielding little more than farm implements and axes. But their spirit has been empowered and enriched by their taste of victory over the Danes at Stamford Bridge.

The bedraggled trio, wet and dripping, know they will have to wait hours before the procession passes, so they slip in a gap just before an approaching herd of pigs can churn the path even more.

"Sire, the men must rest..."

At the head of the column Harold steals an irritable glance at Etheld, one of his closest advisers.

"... Cedric and his men have already collapsed on the track a while back. He refuses to leave his sick and wounded."

Etheld is panting with the effort of making himself heard above the din as he keeps pace with his King, aching feet kicking through a heavy, damp carpet of autumnal leaves which stick to the mud. Here the column is trickling through the forest, barely ten abreast.

"Time a'plenty to put up our feet when we knock at the gates of hell," spits Orfur, the tough, grizzly faced Master of Arms, plunging through the grey drizzle on the King's right.

Harold looks around at the men half running, half striding at his side. He is flanked by his brothers Leofwyne and Gyrth, both cursing and longing for the mounts they cannot ride while their King insists on leading on foot. Their horses, including Edith Swan-neck's, are being led a few paces behind.

"Tell Cedric to take the weakest to the nearest village and join us as soon as he can," Harold tells Etheld. "Send a rider. Tell them we need every able man to keep with the main body. I have no wish to beg William's indulgence while we wait for stragglers."

Harold knows his Yorkshire victory has already done much to stem the incessant tide of terror poured onto his shores from the feared longboats. His faith encourages his men who, through him, sense their immortality and a new, vital role in their country's destiny.

But the fire in their hearts does not spur their feet to Herculean effort, as it does Harold's. He is ablaze with impatience as they barrel back to where they started from, England's southern coast, a stretch of beloved land currently in the Godless clutch of the Duke who burns, pillages and rapes as brutally as any Viking while hungrily awaiting Harold's return.

The sweet taste of victory swiftly turns sour as he marches relentlessly south, daily learning on the hoof of the atrocities committed by William's 8,000 Normans in the hamlets and farmsteads of Sussex.

"My Lord King, my husband," says Edith, concentrating on lifting her brown skirts to avoid the worst of the mud. "I know full well why you walk with the rabble rather than ride."

Her eyes are sparkling with love, even here in the chilly northern rain.

"You are afraid that you will give rein at full gallop and we few will meet the Duke alone on the battlefield, our army left days behind us. But, pray, think of your lady's shoes and suffering feet. The royal cobbler will be kept busy a year hence after this."

Harold turns to look back over his shoulder at the long straggling line behind. After the court's horses, grim-faced men, women and even children stretch as far as the eye can see. Some husbands will not leave their families, even for war.

Edith knows his silence means he is considering her words and she tries to press home her advantage.

"God knows we are travelling with entire kitchens in our train – including toddlers and pets. We are bound to be slow but please let us enjoy the benefit of the saddle from time to time."

Harold looks stern. "Women and children can be a Godsend when it comes to keeping such a massive army running efficiently, especially in camp. They are no burden but it is true I am afraid I shall fly off alone on my steed and face the Normans with my one sword."

When the winding track allows he also catches a glimpse of convoys of handcarts and ox-carts loaded man-height with tents, cooking utensils and weaponry. Several struggle desperately to keep the wooden wheels turning through the thick mud churned to lumpy soup by their sheer numbers.

He has worn his uneasy crown for less than a year – God, when did he last actually wear it, he muses? – and did a king ever have to fight so ferociously to keep it?

Harold now commands a growing force of around 7,000 men, already tired and battle-worn, and further weakened hour-by-hour by their forced march back to the south coast.

But unlike William, he is constantly reinforced at every town and village by freshly invigorated Englishmen quick to sense the patriotic fervour of victory.

It is late afternoon and the rain has finally abated, allowing just the faintest hint of sunshine to enhance the bronze and gold of a forest preparing for winter. A glade before them is alive with cheering villagers, some jumping with joy and waving rough, hand-made flags.

"Long live the King," they shout, louder and louder, but Harold hardly hears them. Without a word he allows them to offer their hospitality.

"Hold the line!"

Harold winces at Orfur's gruff, bellowed order along the line from just an arm's stretch away. His command will be taken up by other men-at-arms and so passed from earshot to earshot. But this shout is far too close to Harold's weary eardrum.

"We'll rest the night here," Harold tells Etheld, "though 'tis barely twilight."

"It is good," replies Etheld. "This will give Cedric time to catch up."

The army is fit to drop and most collapse gratefully when they hear the order to camp, but the villagers are eager to offer what little they can for their hero King and soon a pathetic line of menfolk also jostle and bustle in their haste to enlist.

"Stand orderly, stand orderly," yells Orfur, not above the encouragement of said orderliness with a rough shove on a shoulder or two.

With fatigued eyes Harold surveys the mangy, straggly parade of 15 or so boys and men.

"Village folk like these weren't quite so keen to enlist when we passed through on the way north," Harold confides cynically and quietly to Etheld.

"Nay, sire," agrees Etheld. "There seemed then to be far more pressing matters to attend to; fields to harvest, girls to bed."

"Amazing the power of one kill, in hunting as in war," continues Harold. "Their blood-lust is up. The call to arms is clearly not such a nuisance now they think they are signing up for a march to glory. But look at these waifs… "

Harold walks over and puts his arm around a young boy of about 12 years old.

"I offer you my life, sire," says the boy eagerly in a voice barely broken, dropping to one knee.

"And when you face some Norman knight mounted on a war horse, with what will you fight? A spinning top? A hoop and stick?" The King's voice is kindly, and the boy takes no offence.

Harold lifts him bodily back to his feet and replaces his arm about his shoulders.

The boy regards the scruffy man beside him, smells his sweat and is aware there is not even that much difference in their height.

"Are you... are you really the King?" he asks. "You don't look like a king."

"BOY!" Orfur's stern reprimand barks loudly, but Harold hushes him with a discreet wave of his arm which he then replaces about the boy's shoulder.

"We don't always appear exactly as we are," he tells the boy softly. "For instance, you with your well-scrubbed face and swain's apparel, don't look much like the hero I know you to be."

"If you are indeed the King, where is your crown?" the boy persists.

"Look hard, boy, and you will see it," he replies. "Just as I can see a gleaming sword raised above your head, ready to strike at England's enemy. Just as I can see the courage shining from a young face that hasn't yet needed the benefit of a shave."

The boy is quiet for a moment. Then his eyes gleam as he says: "I can see it. I can see your crown. Take me with you to fight the Normans. I can page for you too."

"Your place is best here with your mother," Harold murmurs quietly. "Someone has got to keep the village running while we see off the invader. That's a man's job too."

He senses as much as sees the soft smile and the palpable relief of a woman standing nearby, her hands clasped before her like a supplicant.

"Sire... " the boy begins, but the King hushes him with a paternal slap on the back and wheels him towards his mother. She is silent but gratitude pours from her eyes, a message clearer than any of Orfur's barkings.

Nonetheless as he gives his last-minute instructions to his commanders, he is startled again when Orfur loudly repeats the command. The message is taken up by another, and another, all the way through the camp.

Orfur looks at him expectantly and Harold dismisses him curtly, too tired for manners. Orfur walks to his horse, mounts and sets off to do his rounds.

He returns within the hour to find the royal court already ensconced around the marquee with pennants flying proud.

Etheld is quietly playing his flute but stops when a messenger whispers in his ear.

"Sire," Etheld tells the King, "Cedric has sent word that he will bring his wounded here. He hopes to arrive before dawn and fully expects to march with us at daybreak."

The King is hardly listening, staring into the fire as if the future of England can be foreseen in the red, orange and yellow flames. Sparks from the crackling, damp wood rush up eagerly to join the stars that shine like diamonds in a cloudless night sky.

Edith comes up to stand behind him, one hand resting lightly on his shoulder.

"All will be well," she coaxes soothingly. "See how the fire dances with joy. Its warmth is our warmth – it has taken us to its heart."

Harold smiles and pats her hand.

"And I am to suppose that William is right now trying to warm his blood-stained fingers over cold, friendless flames?"

"He is... if it is raining in Sussex," she insists. "And it always is. The flames in our fire are spreading and leaping eagerly to the bough – just as our people are rushing now to join you, their valiant, victorious King."

Etheld puts down his flute and politely clears his throat for attention.

"We may be weary, sire, but our numbers grow rapidly as your lady describes. Every day on the march, every town and every village, brings us more and more willing conscripts."

Harold nods submissively. "Yet my sleep serves only to perpetuate the horrors, and my dreams are merely nightmares sent by William to torment me. Every second wasted like this cuts me to the quick."

He buries his tormented face in his hands as he adds: "I wish I had some magic spell that would transport us to the battlefield this very instant."

* * * * *

"My God, the devil himself has been set loose here," seethes Orfur as he cuts down the body of a half-naked woman hanging upside down in the truck of a charred handcart. Mercifully, she is long-since dead but the brutal work of her torturers is there for all to see.

A VICTORY /OURED

It is already October and Harold has finally reached Sussex and is sickened by the carnage. Farms and villages are burned to the ground, peasants slaughtered by the dozen. A fevered hatred eats at his soul and he plans to make at once for the perfect battleground, a Sussex escarpment which will become known as Harold's Hill.

"We'll take the high ground quickly, before 8,000 Norman arses soil the hilltop," spits Harold, urging his footsore men ever forward. He can hardly bear wait a second more for his broadsword to seek out the soft flesh beneath Norman chain mail.

His commanders know better than to argue, and they too are shocked by the unremitting horror visited on the land by the merciless marauder.

Harold Godwinson does not want to rest, neither does he even need to, but his men are mortal and rest they must. This moonlit night he allows them to embrace the jubilant, noisy welcome of another small village where wine and food is passionately offered.

"No wine!" orders Harold. "We march on our feet and our feet must stay true to the ground." Nonetheless he knows some may ignore the command.

His thoughts race as fast as his heart. Seven thousand men – about the size of a Roman legion – but unlike that invading war machine of 1,000 years earlier, his men know little of the value of discipline.

He watches dispassionately as a young girl of about 11 stands in awe and terror before one of the Viking conscripts that have now joined their number. The man Va'ard – as Harold knows him to be – had been an important captain in the defeated Danish invasion force. He looms menacingly like a towering giant, half as tall again as many men, and broad like a barrel.

His long, hairy furs are filthy and matted with the reds and browns of battle and their forced march, the hairs partly concealing the fearsome double bladed axe tucked in his belt. But the little girl sees enough to chill her to the bone, for Harold knows this is the vision she has been carefully taught to dread – a Viking in full battledress.

The King half smiles as he sees her tiptoe carefully but curiously towards the Viking, one small nervous step followed by another, until she is close enough to reach out and touch his long, straggly beard.

Va'ard's steely blue eyes watch her as he would a scared rabbit or doe. Then, just as her fingers dare reach up to the stringy grey-white of his beard, he rears up to his full height and girth and lets out a bellow that would have impressed Thor himself.

The little girl's parents run laughing to lift her from the ground as fright sends her sprawling and screaming across the grass.

"Hush, girl, 'tis a friend," smiles her father, but he too keeps one careful eye on the fearsome Dane who now stands grinning from one battle-scarred ear to the other.

Harold turns away and catches the glance of his trusted l ieutenant Orfur.

"See the men have a mind more for sleep than merriment," he orders. But in truth his exhausted army needs no such command. Neither wine nor warm, willing women can lure most of them back from the twilight of their half-life fatigue.

Harold too is near fit to collapse, but it is his rage that keeps him going, his inexhaustible fury as the Normans plunder, rape and pillage his homeland..

He has only one burning ambition: to plunge his avenging sword into William's breast. He is blind to all else.

But deep inside he knows the men must lay down their heads occasionally lest their bellowing snores, he reflects, be all they have to despatch William to the pits of hell.

"Discipline is what we lack," Harold tells Orfur and his adjutants later that night around a roaring fire.

"That's the weapon the Romans visited upon us and which brought us to our knees, a millennium ago. Not their dreaded fireball trebuchets, not their bathhouses and underfloor heating which indeed mollycoddled and sapped the will out of us all; no, it was their discipline."

Orfur is not a learned man, but he knows enough to nod vigorously whenever the King speaks, especially if he is in full flow like tonight.

"Discipline doesn't sound much like William's main strength," he ventures. "Not the way he's letting his men run amok in Sussex while he waits for us."

The sudden reminder saddens Harold. He knows also that Orfur may be completely wrong about that.

Harold has had first-hand experience of William's court, himself a 'guest' there after being shipwrecked two years earlier. He is aware that it is widely believed that he 'gratefully' promised William the Crown of England in exchange for his safekeeping and hospitality then. It was an unfortunate episode that he prefers to forget, and Harold keeps it locked away deep inside.

He sees himself as a good king, a truthful king, a great believer in the Golden Age of Arthurian legend when the Knights of the Round Table righted wrongs and upheld all that was truth and justice.

He yearns more than anything to see England return to that time of grace, and for the world to witness that it was by his inspired rule – Harold's – that this rebirth was engineered. His England is an industrious, potentially wealthy nation that needs only a strong guiding hand to once more retrieve the gleaming sword of Excalibur from the stone. He wants to be that guiding hand, that Arthur, that once and future king.

Once again laughing knights like the blue-eyed Sir Lancelot shall ride the land on fine mounts, overseeing the new, shining realm and displaying to the world that Old Englande will have no truck with despots or tyrants.

He fervently believes that a little white lie told to ensure his safekeeping whilst on foreign shores is wholeheartedly in keeping with the spirit of the Round Table.

"Discipline," he tells the roaring fire suddenly, warming his hands near its flames. "That is the weapon that will win the day in Sussex, discipline."

Gyrth and Leofwyne tend to keep their counsel. Both are unambitious men happy to allow their brother to lead and to steal the glory. Harold loves them both fiercely and remembers that as he studies their faces in the firelight.

"Grace favoured us at Stamford Bridge," says Leofwyne quietly. "Whatever it is we may lack, it didn't assist the Vikings so I see no reason for it to do any more for the Normans."

LUDEC

"I'll make sure the men are turned in," says Orfur and rises to his feet.

* * * * *

On the other side of the camp reluctant warrior Ludec turns over in his blanket for the hundredth time. He can see the embers of his own fire beginning to fade and die and the cold starts to cut into him like steel. Exhausted and limp though he is, he cannot find the comfort of sleep. The ground is chilly and lumpy beneath his aching body.

His chief concern is his wife Astrid, whom he has abandoned at their Sussex farmstead in her eighth month of pregnancy. Astrid – with her uncannily piercing blue eyes – is his entire life. But though he longs to be with her, neither does he want his son or daughter born to be an invader's slave.

His king's preoccupation with revenge worries him, and he is convinced that running headlong back into battle so soon after their last is not the wisest way. But he is a farmer's son, not even a regular soldier, so who would ever listen to him? Still, he recognises the dangers, and fears for Astrid, his unborn child, his king and his country. His very absence from home feels like a betrayal.

He is also concerned that he is getting an unsavoury and unwarranted reputation among his warrior colleagues for what they see as an unwillingness for the coming battle.

He tries once more to settle his aching body on the cold, uncomfortable ground. Sleep still does not come. His memory replays with agitation his earlier conversation with Steg.

"I'm not saying we shouldn't fight," he had said. "Only that rushing like lambs to the slaughter like this may not be so clever."

"It is the King's wish and thereby it is our duty," Steg had replied, guardedly. "Even if we do think we've got better things to attend to, like your pregnant wife, and my cows and corn."

"Have you ever heard of Arminius?" Ludec went on, warming to his subject. Ludec was a farmer's son but prosperous by the standards of the day and unusually well read.

"Not this side of Friday," retorted Steg defensively.

"History talkers tell of a young rebel from Germania who united the tribes east of the Rhine to give the Romans a bloody nose, shortly before Caesar conquered England," explained Ludec.

"Then we can do it to the Normans – like we did to the Vikings. Eventually." Steg added the last word mutedly, after a thoughtful pause.

"Yes, but Arminius was educated in Rome, taught to think like a Roman, taught to feel like a Roman, but when it came down to it he didn't fight like a Roman. He knew better."

"Wait a bit," Steg had said, confused. "I thought he was from Germania?"

"He was. A tribal chief's son. But he was taken by the Romans as a sort of hostage. It was usual practice in those days. Given a Roman education, taught to 'be' a Roman. It was their way of getting important foreigners to spread the word."

"Except that he did not?" Steg had caught on.

"Except that he did not," confirmed Ludec. "He used the forests of his homeland to thwart the Roman war machine. Turtle formations, war towers and trebuchets are useless in woods thick with oak, no matter how many you can line up in a pretty row."

"William hasn't got trebuchets," Steg pointed out, confused again.

"No, but he has heavy horses, thousands and thousands of them. A formidable weapon, each horse done up like a monster in chain mail and protected by projecting metal spikes. We're going to have to face unstoppable formations of them... "

Ludec waited until he could see the unpleasant picture etch itself firmly into Steg's reasoning.

Then he added: "But horses are next to useless in thick woodland; easy to ambush and completely unable to climb trees like men."

Steg's face burst alight with wonder, his very own epiphany.

"We could give William a bloody nose, just like Harmonious."

"Arminius," corrected Ludec.

"He was a good man, that Arminius. What happened to him?"

"Oh, I think he was eventually beheaded or skewered to death. Something equally dreadful."

He watched with amusement as Steg's face returned to its usual state of non-comprehension before he got up to turn in.

"All I'm saying is: there's more than one way to win a fight. Some would say we were lucky at Stamford Bridge – we caught them by surprise. But William's got our King well and truly biting at the bit and now he's ready and waiting for us."

"With several thousand heavy horses," added Steg sombrely. "All chain-mailed and armed with metal spikes pointing out at our eyeballs."

"Don't listen to him," a voice yelled from the darkness. "That Ludec's a pansy who wants to get home to his woman. Just because she's with foal."

"Wouldn't mind that myself," called out another, coarse and chuckling crudely. "She's quite tasty, by all accounts."

Ludec had pulled the blanket over his ears to try to block out these ugly taunts. It was hard to believe that these men were on his side, his own countrymen.

Now he lays there still, fighting not for his life but for sleep, knowing the former challenge will come soon enough.

* * * * *

Ludec averts his eyes as he passes the corpse of a toddler girl, no more than 4 years old, laying naked and butchered on her dead mother's breast.

Both mother and child had been sexually mutilated, their blood mingling as one. Ludec prays that they met an early death and that they didn't watch each other suffer, but is haunted by what he suspects to be the unpalatable truth.

He can hardly scramble on through the undergrowth, his sight blinkered by a heavy veil of tears.

In Sussex, the exhausted army is surrounded by evidence of the massacres they have been hearing about all the way south. Horrific scenes of slaughtered villages – girls and young children raped and hanging naked to further enrage Harold. In some outlying farms, entire families and their livestock have had their throats cut – probably with the same blades, man and beast.

They pass through these cameos of carnage more and more frequently as they close on Harold's chosen battleground.

Harold is incensed and screams uncontrollably as he rushes onward towards revenge. But on that evening of October 13 with the army camped a stone's throw from the chosen battlefield Ludec decides it is time to stand up and be counted.

His face stern and resolved, Ludec sets his private plan in motion and strides confidently to the King's encampment.

"I need to talk to the King," he tells a guard at the edge of the Royal Reserve. The guard looks at him with a cold contempt that scares him even more than the oncoming battle.

"See your captain," replies the guard, brusque, dismissive.

"I've tried that. He won't listen to me."

The guard smiles and relaxes a little. He leans on his spear. This is going to be easy.

"Then what makes you think the King wants to harken to you if your captain doesn't?"

Orfur is passing at that moment, only mildly curious until another voice cries out: "Don't listen to him – he's a snivelling wimp. He just wants to go home."

This opportunity of a little bullying excites him and he steps over the mud to Ludec and the guard.

"Want to go home, eh?" His voice is deceptively smooth. He senses a kill and seductively urges him to speak. Even with the muck and grime of several days' marching, it is obvious from Ludec's apparel that he is not from peasant stock. The sneering officer is not impressed but Ludec is no fool.

"I want to be nowhere but at my King's side," Ludec says quickly. "But I need to talk to him urgently."

"He's a coward," says a ruffian with a short sword in his belt, and jostles him violently as he passes.

"That's Ludec, William's louse," shouts another, and Ludec realises with growing dismay the voices are getting angrier.

"Sniveller," jeers someone else. "God knows who put a spark in your woman's belly. Can't have been you."

The guard and Orfur are becoming more and more interested, but for all the wrong reasons. Orfur is snarling and towers over him menacingly, so close Ludec can smell the gruel on his breath.

He has tried to speak to the King on several occasions but so far official channels have got him nowhere.

Now his desperate, full-frontal attack is failing miserably too, the guard and Orfur treating him more like an enemy than an ally. Accusing stares seem to throw chains around his entire body, moment by moment. It won't be long, he feels, before he is hurled into some makeshift dungeon... or worse.

The final straw comes from Steg, drawn to the scene by all the commotion.

"That's Ludec," he shouts, pointing excitedly. His adrenaline is flooding beyond control in the blood-lust of the baying crowd. "He's been telling me about this Roman traitor called Harmonious who betrayed his men by climbing up a tree on a horse."

The guard and Orfur exchange a decisive glance and then grab Ludec roughly by the shoulders, bundling him back towards the Royal Tent.

"I think the King should be told of this tale-spinning traitor," says Orfur and Ludec can feel a chill stab at the pit of his stomach.

He hears loud, urgent shouts as Orfur leaves him in the watchful clutches of the guard and crosses to the King's tent.

Petrified, Ludec fears for his life and yearns to see Astrid's face before him, smiling and welcoming, instead of this ocean of hostility. He looks around in panic and sees nothing but sneers and accusation.

"Bring him forward!" The voice is Orfur's, chillingly familiar but now without a trace of comradeship.

He is pushed unceremoniously through the flaps of the Royal Tent and sees the King before him. Dry mouthed in fear, he struggles hard to swallow, grimly aware that this may be his darkest hour.

Harold stands there, magnificent, even in his muddied battle attire. Twice as old as the 22-year-old Ludec, his face wise and grim. Ludec recognises two other men in the tent, Harold's brothers Gyrth and Leofwyne. They survey him dispassionately, their arms folded. There too is Edith Swan-neck and Etheld.

"You want to go home, I hear?" says Harold, solicitously. "The sound of battle getting a little too close for comfort?" He smiles directly at him, but it is false and insincere, devoid of warmth.

"Sire, think me not a coward," he pleads when he is shoved forward yet again, this time stumbling to his knees. "Yet I feel there is a need here for caution and patience."

The King and his commanders visibly wince at such weakling words, and it is all Harold can do to stop his chief adjutants from slicing him from crown to chin as he kneels before him.

"Let him speak before he dies," he says, holding his hand to stay the executioners.

"My King... " begins Ludec, trembling and hesitant.

CHAPTER TWO

HIDE AND SEEK

With a shaking hand, Ludec wipes droplets of stinging perspiration from his eyes. He knows beyond all doubt he has made the biggest misjudgement of his young life. He looks up at the unfriendly faces all around him, and longs to see Astrid one last time before he dies.

Even on this chilly night he is sweating from the claustrophobic heat of four crackling torches in the great tent. The moment seems eternal. Harold is watching Etheld who is watching Orfur who, sword drawn, is snarling down at Ludec sprawled on his knees on the floor.

"Sire," says Etheld. "This boy has come to your court of his own free will. That alone takes courage. I pray thee, call off your hounds."

Harold nods almost imperceptibly to Orfur who reluctantly re-sheaths his blade, but not before putting his right foot to Ludec's shoulder for a final, brutal kick. Ludec is aware that it is small compensation for not being allowed to slit his throat.

Ludec winces and rubs the bruise. Harold turns away from the scene as if bored and stares straight into the eyes of his Lady Edith. Even Gyrth and Leofwyne relax a little.

"Speak," the King demands of Ludec. "I want my supper and my bed."

"My King, I know that we do battle on the morrow against the despot Norman Duke," Ludec begins cautiously. "But I beg thee to consider why it is that William is wreaking such terror upon the land all about us."

The King appears to be listening. Ludec's voice grows bolder.

HIDE AND JEEK

"Why does he burn the very fields that he himself must depend upon to eat, as must we? Could it be, my Lord, that the invader is a little too desperate for combat? Could it be he knows his only chance of success is to fight here and now before our numbers get too strong?"

His words tumble on, to fill the ensuing silence.

"Forgive me, sire, for my presumption. I am no military strategist. But the Duke can deploy on the field only those who stand beside him now. He can eat only what he steals, without benefit of reinforcements or supplies in this, to him, hostile terrain.

"Respectfully, good King, I fear he may be deliberately goading us into early confrontation. That is the reason for all the bloodshed and terror inflicted on our helpless villagers. He knows that hour by hour our supplies are being replenished by willing countrymen and women and that our forces swell daily."

He has been neither shushed nor slain, so Ludec dares to continue.

"He is also aware that we are as tired as wearied wraiths after our recent victorious battle, and our long forced march back to the southlands. He knows he must strike now, while we are enfeebled."

Ludec draws hope from the King's attentive stance, a thoughtful finger to his chin.

"He cannot restock, he cannot reinforce. Every day that passes he is the one getting weaker while we can only get stronger. I beg thee, sire, do not take to sword too early. That is his greatest will – to lure us into a premature battle when we have everything to gain by waiting, and he has everything to lose."

Harold is still gazing into Edith's eyes, lost in his own thoughts. In the silence, Ludec hears the echo of his own outrageous outspokenness, disturbed only by the spitting flames of the torches.

Finally Harold turns from Edith and stares down at the boy.

"And what do we tell the fathers and mothers of the children we see ripped limb from limb by the Norman demon? Do we say, pray excuse us, but we must hide in the woods awhile where it is safe and warm?"

Ludec drops his eyes to the floor. This is a question to which he has no answer.

Again the assembled court can only wait in silence as the King shuffles back and forth, clearly in dilemma. Every minute feels like an hour to Ludec who curses his own arrogance at daring to question the wisdom of kings. Finally Harold approaches him, and Ludec can feel no enmity.

The King looks at him a long while, his face creased with the heavy burden of leadership. Suddenly his shoulders, that had started to hunch, straighten and there is a new look in his eye. Something fresh, something alive.

"Stand," he commands and Ludec shuffles awkwardly to his feet, still nursing his right shoulder blade.

Harold stares at him. "Where are you from?"

"Alvriceston, sire. I run a farmstead there. It was my father's, and his father's before him."

"My Lord, he is an impertinent knave," blusters Orfur. "His woman is with child and he yearns only to be with her. He has no stomach for battle."

"He stood not with us at Stamford Bridge?"

Orfur looks at his feet, lost for words.

"Was he not craving for his woman and unborn child then?"

Harold turns to face Ludec directly and places his hand on his right shoulder. Ludec winces at the reminder of his bruises.

"You are young," he tells him after a pause. "Yet perhaps wise beyond your years. It may be that England shall find itself in your debt because of your thoughtful counsel."

Ludec is stunned. He has already forgotten the ache in his shoulder. He catches Lady Edith's glance and detects the faintest trace of a smile on her lips.

The King begins to pace in a courtly fashion, addressing the company in general. Ludec senses that what he has said seems to have inspired a speech the King is now framing and rehearsing inside his head.

"The Norse beast has been slain and shall never again harry the shores of Old Englande, their horned helm lies broke and rent asunder. When the Normans are defeated we shall re-visit their quaking kinsfolk in the north and pay our respects for centuries of bloodshed.

"Meanwhile I have decided we shall indeed tarry, for it is true that we get mightier with every new day dawning, while William can only get weaker. Battle can wait."

It is a difficult decision for Harold, the images of slaughter they have all witnessed preying uppermost on all their minds. But Ludec's words have revealed to him the evil intent behind William's sadistic strategy.

Harold informs his commanders that tomorrow, when they would have marched to battle, they will melt instead into the woods.

"These are the beloved forests we know so well and where William treads as a stranger – he will never find us," he tells them.

Orfur again lowers his eyes to signify respectful opposition but Etheld speaks for him.

"Perhaps wise, my King," he says. "But the men are baying like hounds to make William pay for his savagery. We will need all our powers of persuasion to convince them otherwise."

The King waves a dismissive hand. His mind is made up and all else is of no consequence.

"Bring your belongings here," he tells Ludec. Turning to Orfur he adds: "Arrange a tent for him near the court and make him comfortable. "

"Sire, I... " Ludec is too shocked to speak but the King hushes him anyway.

"Where best to hide an army, young Ludec?" he asks conspiratorially as Orfur obediently ducks out of the Royal Tent to see to his wishes.

"The forests about Alvriceston are thick and hilly," Ludec replies. "If we camp on the high ground, we can post sentries in the trees and evade discovery forever should we wish."

"You know these forests, of course."

"Like the back of my hand, sire."

"Then you shall help choose the spot. You may stay close to my court but I warn you, I shall not be good company. There is much blood and guilt wed to what we are doing. It may well be William's evil intention to provoke us, but his actions burn like an arrow aflame nonetheless."

"I fear that he will continue to maim and kill," concedes Ludec. "But if we defy him and wait we will be sure to wreak the final revenge we all yearn for. The only problem will be if William decides instead to march directly on London."

"I have considered that," says the King. "In that case we must leave the forest and stalk him all the way, only closing for battle when he is stuck between us and the city walls. But, mark my word, that won't happen. It's me he wants. I'm his chief preoccupation as he is mine."

That night Ludec relaxes on a camp-bed in a fine tent close enough to the Royal Court to hear the last snippets of conversation before sleep.

Loudest of all he can hear Orfur in a tent nearby, disgruntled and grumbling about Ludec's surprise influence over matters that, in his eyes, he knows nothing about.

"Naturally he wants to hide in the forest at Friston because that's where his pregnant wench is," he is whispering to someone. "But while the King hesitates, Sussex is butchered. That Ludec is nought but a sniveller. He would see Old Englande under the iron yoke and, yay, happily shear his head like a sheep."

Ludec pulls up the blanket and tries to ignore Orfur's angry jibes, content with his change of fortune but fully aware his troubles are not yet over. Orfur's tirade has heightened his fears and what if Astrid becomes another victim of the marauding Normans?

He shuts his eyes tight against the horrific images he had seen earlier – a young woman straddled and strapped across the back of a cart, her bloodied body mutilated and raped.

He dreams troubled dreams of playing cat-and-mouse in the woods, desperately climbing trees to try to spot Astrid a few short miles away.

* * * * *

At that very moment Astrid is being taken west by her worried father. She has no choice but to succumb to his will but as she sways first this way and then that on the bumpy wagon she holds her swollen belly in her hands and prays to her Christian God that Ludec will be spared in the bloodshed to come.

Her father has a cousin, Beatrice, on the Isle of Wit. Egbert thinks they will be safer there.

But as she flees to safety, it is Astrid who feels like the betrayer.

* * * * *

The next day brings a fine, clear autumnal morning. Ludec is among the Royal Court at the head of the column as they make for the safety of the deep, dark forest.

At one point Orfur draws up next to him on a proud, snorting stallion. As he pulls on the reins to control his impatient beast he sneers down at Ludec.

"Congratulations, you now appear to rank as one of the King's advisers," he barks. "But how can you hope to fare with men who were trained to kill before they were taught to walk? My father was a warrior, an officer in Edward's army, and his father before him. Brought up with the sword.

"I care not a tad for your cowardly strategies and even less for you. I'll be watching you, boy. Your fancy words may win you a silk tent under which to hide your lying tongue, but you don't fool me. I'll be watching you."

Aware that others nearby are coming within earshot, Orfur nudges his horse with an incoherent yell and gallops away forward of the line.

Ludec rides on, eyes front, keeping his own counsel. His so-called former comrades don't come anywhere near him anymore.

By the end of the day they have chosen a strategic camp hidden deep in the woods and on high ground. Sentries are posted in the treetops and Harold's army disappears into oblivion as if it never existed.

Ludec is desperate to head to Alvriceston to see Astrid, still unaware that she is no longer there, but after just a week everyone's nerves are frayed. While Ludec worries over his wife, the King is riddled with guilt as stories pour in of continuing massacres.

"It is as if the Norman Duke wants to extinguish all life in Sussex," a breathless messenger tells the King. "Nothing is spared – no building, no stock. Even babies are left to rot where they are slain, their eyes pecked out by the crows."

Ludec is nearby and listening. He sees Orfur ostensibly tending to some menial task in the camp and is shocked to see that he is, as he warned, watching him. He feels like a spy and shifts uneasily.

But Ludec tears himself away from Orfur's accusing gaze and instead studies the King's creased countenance. He can read the torment and remorse in his eyes and his furrowed brow, and knows his own counsel is the cause.

"Curse the dark dungeon of this forest – I feel like a prisoner behind tall wooden bars," splutters the King angrily. "Curse that damned Norman heathen too. Would that the crows peck out his black heart."

"Fear not," a gentle voice whispers in Ludec's ear. It is Etheld who has also noticed the furtive figure of Orfur lurking just out of earshot. "The King is distraught as are we all. But he blames you not. You are the voice of reason and he knows it."

With his eyes and in silence, Ludec tries to convey his thanks for his kindness. Then they both turn back to continue to listen attentively to the messenger.

"William knows he has been thwarted, and is driven insane by fury," he goes on. "He marched on our last known position only to find we had vanished into the night like wizards. Now he wreaks his revenge on any peace-loving farmstead and land worker he happens upon. Blood smears the fertile fields of Sussex bright crimson."

Finally Orfur makes an impassioned plea to Harold to let him take out a small patrol to spy on William's movements and strengths.

"Corpses are the only crops sown in Sussex this year," he tells the King. "Our kinsfolk are being skewered by the Duke's spears while we hide in the woods. Let me at least scout his strength without leading him back to our main force."

Harold reluctantly agrees and Orfur steals out at the dead of night with 50 horsed men and circles William's troops to approach him from the north-east so as not to reveal Harold's true position in the north-west if spotted.

What they see horrifies even the hardened Housecarls. Scenes of unrivalled butchery sicken them all, including the tough Viking conscripts.

HIDE AND SEEK

Orfur watches his second-in-command Rufus the Red cut down a man bound to a tree just outside a burning hamlet. It is night-time.

"He's still alive – he's trying to say something," says Rufus, laying him as comfortably as he can on the ground beside their horses. "His lips are moving."

Orfur starts to laugh as the man's mouth slowly eases open to reveal the head of a small rat poking out from between the man's blood-stained teeth. The rat's nose twitches, uncertain, before scampering away across the grass from his interrupted meal of intestines and liver.

Rufus, who has dropped the man's head from his cradled arms in shock, turns to look up at Orfur on his horse. He is further sickened to see the expression he reads on his face.

For all the horror, Orfur still can't hide his secret triumph. "A rat!" he screams, almost demented. "What a 'tail' he had to tell!"

Nearby one of the battle-hardened Viking conscripts turns away to retch violently into the grass.

"See, soon there will be nothing left of our fair land to defend," says Orfur, climbing down from his horse to stare in disbelief at more piles of broken, torn bodies in the entirely razed hamlet. Buildings and corpses burn all around them, filling their nostrils with an intolerable stench.

Rufus wipes away a rare, secretive tear from his bearded, dirt-encrusted face.

"The boy's right, Orfur," he says. "There's only one reason for all this butchery. William wants us to take him on now, on his terms. It is wisdom to wait."

"At risk of losing every man, woman and child we've ever loved," spits Orfur just as a shower of arrows noiselessly takes down several in their patrol. It is dark but Orfur and Rufus can clearly see the men dropping like dogs in the moonlight and flames. There is not a single scream.

"To sword!" they yell and rush on foot through the trees towards the archers. They have been surprised by a patrol of Norman foragers and fight desperately against twice their number, many on heavy horses and chain mailed.

Their blades slash indiscriminately in panic this way and that, their only recourse against greater odds to fight like berserkers. Orfur howls like a wolf as he confronts two, three Norman archers at a time, his blade glinting ferociously in the moonlight like a mad moonbeam.

For a moment Rufus is forced to stand his ground before two formidable Norman war horses, their chain-mailed riders both holding heavyweight maces with two hands above their heads. They are menacingly poised, ready to strike. It looks like the end for Rufus.

Suddenly, like a gazelle, he darts under the belly of the nearest beast and thrusts his blade deep into its underbelly, before dashing out again to escape its threshing hooves. The horse rears, whimpering in pain, and then collapses into the flank of the second. Both riders tumble heavily to the ground, their weighty maces half burying themselves uselessly in the mud.

Rufus plunges his bloodied sword into first one, and then the second Norman as they desperately, clumsily try to get back on their feet.

Mounted Norman escorts behind the archers struggle to join the melee, such is the press of dead and dying, and Orfur's men use the confusion to slip away back into the woods. Once out of range of the light from the blazing outhouses, Rufus and Orfur cease their battle yells and become as silent as the fox.

They have lost many comrades but they slip away into the night and head, as planned, towards the north-east away from their main camp. Their horses are lighter and faster than the mounts of their Norman pursuers and even in the dark they can fly at full gallop across terrain they know far better than the enemy.

Eventually, when they are sure they are no longer followed, they swing around to the west and finally drift back to camp at dawn, wiser and more cautious men.

"They are a brutal and well-armed force," Orfur tells the King. But it is nothing they don't already know.

Harold turns to Etheld.

"The more I hear the more I know the boy is right," he says quietly. "Only vastly superior numbers will drive these devils from our fields."

HIDE AND SEEK

Some weeks later messengers bring more news. Firstly Ludec hears from his village about Astrid's forcible departure to the west.

"Her father took her," explains the messenger. "The folk at the village knew not where. A relative perhaps? Whatever his plan he had to drag her. She didn't care to go."

At Christmas Harold learns that the Normans have been sent reinforcements, a small flotilla of 12 ships but which have all mercifully foundered under easterly storms.

"Fierce gales have blown everything they can't destroy onto the shores of the Isle of Wit," reports a rider.

"Nobody seems to know whether the surviving Normans there pose a threat or not. They may be a spent force or they may at this very moment be regrouping and planning to continue their ravages on the island. Sire, the news is still unclear."

Ludec buries his face in his hands. He wishes he knew whether Astrid has made it to safety.

To Etheld he bemoans: "I too can only sit it out in these wintry woods and wait and worry. It is torture the equal of any William could inflict on me."

But the King becomes more and more heartened as fresh reinforcements pour in almost daily, swelling their numbers to over 15,000 strong.

They come from as far away as Scotland, from the capital known in later times as Wallaceburn, and this very day they are joined by a well-armed and horsed contingent of Druids from the west country.

"Pretty soon these woods won't be big enough to hide us all," he jokes to Ludec and Etheld in the Royal Tent, where Ludec has become a regular guest.

"You will join us for our Yuletide feast of venison, young Ludec. It is a command not a request. And then after dining we shall discuss our plans for William's Christmas present."

He laughs heartily and Ludec feels good that he alone has been responsible for the King's lighter spirit.

They had waited as he advised and now they were twice as strong, twice as certain of victory.

But as Harold worries about a renegade force of shipwrecked Normans venting their revenge for the English weather on the Isle of Wit's peaceful inhabitants, Ludec's heart aches for Astrid.

Then late on Christmas Day, Ludec is there when the King greets a rider from Alvriceston.

"With your permission, sire, I have bad news for Ludec," he says and turns from the King to face him. "Your wife's father – he has taken her to the Isle of Wit, where the Norman reinforcements were shipwrecked."

Ludec simply stares at him, barely able to believe his ears.

CHAPTER THREE
DEATH'S DOMINION

2nd January 1067: The Battle of Hastings

William awakes on this crisp, frosty morning to a commotion outside his tent. His restless army is camped, waiting, on the same hill that Harold had picked out for the oncoming battle, and upon which William has promised to build himself a proud, magnificent abbey after victory.

"My Lord Duke! Urgent news."

Irritably, William instructs the messenger to enter, buckling on his chain mail vest as he does so.

The soldier stands breathless before him. "Harold has come out of hiding. Scouts report he left the woods at dawn and is heading this way."

"Strength?" demands the Duke.

"The patrol estimates around 5,000. Perhaps 100 horses, no more."

William looks triumphant and strokes the stubble on his chin. There will be no time for a shave today.

"Très bien," he mutters to himself. "Now we have him. We shall crush the pretender as he crawls like a snail from his shell – his men have deserted him to cry over their charred fields and chattels."

With a noisy clatter of scabbard and armour the Duke is joined in the tent by other officers, awaiting instructions.

"We march within the hour," he commands. "Make ready."

Some miles away high on another downland hill the six-man patrol that broke the news is still keeping watch from their hiding place.

"Sacré coeur!" exclaims their leader, suddenly. "Look to the east!"

There, a mile or two further around the perimeter of the woods, another body of men is emerging from the trees. At first they look like a dozen or so stragglers. But then they count 100...1,000... 2,000... and still they keep coming.

"And there!" comes another shout, and they follow his gaze westward; more men pouring from the woods at a point two miles the other way.

Before long they are staring in disbelief at three separate armies each of around 5,000 men in strength. It is a trap and they know if William reacts to their earlier report and marches on the first army he will be caught in a classic pincer movement.

"Ride like the wind," the leader commands. "Warn William before he is outflanked."

Deep in the valley the Duke is alerted just in time by the panting, sweating rider. He is but five miles from joining battle.

"Retournons au camp," he sighs. "We will march back to the hill and keep to the high ground. Even with 50,000 men Harold will not breach us there, armed with nothing but pitchforks and a string of market ponies."

* * * * *

Astrid lies panting rapidly on a cot in a small, rough-stone crofter's cottage on the Isle of Wit.

"There, there, girl," soothes the motherly, red-cheeked woman, as she repeatedly wrings out a wet cloth and places it on Astrid's perspiring forehead.

The woman is Astrid's father's cousin Beatrice and shares Astrid's fears that he will not return in time from the village with the midwife. Beatrice has only once before helped deliver a child and that was tragically still-born. She keeps this information to herself.

"He'll be back soon. He's taken the fastest horse. Speedier than lightning, Old Black."

Suddenly a scuffling at the cottage door alerts the women. Standing there in the open doorway are two enormous chain-mailed Norman knights, stooping under the low, wood-beamed lintel. They shuffle together uneasily.

For a moment both women are shocked by their presence, even without their helmets they can't disguise their menacing, war-like stature. A shiver of involuntary fear runs through them both.

"Logs are finished, madame," says one, in halting English. "Chopped good."

"Thank you, Claude," murmurs Beatrice. "But for God's sake get some different clothing. You scare the wits out of us."

"We have nothing. All lost with the ships," he replies and even in his glinting chain mail still manages to look pathetic. "Mademoiselle is... close to birthing?"

Beatrice nods and fails to hide her growing panic. "We're waiting for the midwife, now."

Astrid's piercing blue eyes are following the scene but not the conversation. She is delirious with pain.

"La douleur est régulière? The pain is... regular?" Claude has stepped forward a few paces into the room, making Beatrice a little uncomfortable. Astrid's expression is too vague to know if she cares.

"Like a drum-beat," replies Beatrice. "Could be any moment now. God, I hope Egbert finds help soon. I fear it may be... a difficult birth."

Claude can clearly see she is distressed.

He is one of some 150 survivors of the storms that destroyed William's flotilla of would-be Christmas reinforcements, washed up bedraggled and helpless on the island's beaches.

The islanders treated them just like any other shipwrecked souls, offering shelter, medical aid and food. They were well aware of the Norman invasion 100 miles or so to the east at Pevensey, but these men in these circumstances were entirely divorced from it. They were simply shipwrecked sailors, and the islanders had seen their share of those.

The Normans themselves responded in kind. The islanders had literally saved many of their lives. There was no war here, just gratitude.

"Madame," he begins. "Mon amie est une guerisseuse. Mon amie my ship's healer woman. She too survived the rocks. She will know something of midwifery... I fetch?"

Beatrice looks at him a moment, uncertain. It could be hours before Egbert arrives back. It could be too late. Beatrice is scared.

"Pray do," she says quietly. Then repeats herself much louder so there can be no doubt. "PRAY DO! Egbert has taken the mare but there is an old piebald grazing at the back. She's better than nothing. But please HURRY!"

Claude doesn't hesitate another moment and rushes out to find the nag.

* * * * *

Harold pounds his open palm with his fist.

"This is what I mean by lack of discipline. I told Gyrth and Leofwyne to wait until I sent word before they emerged from the woods. We would have snared him snug and smart."

"I believe they may have panicked when they saw William was on the move." Etheld looks apologetic as if it were entirely his fault. "They fear only for you, sire."

"They didn't obey my orders. That is exactly what will lose us wars," rants Harold. "They are a baying, unruly mob – listen to them, you can hear them from here."

They stop their column for a moment and sure enough a roar like screaming banshees pounds in their ears from two directions. Gyrth and Leofwyne are leading their respective armies at a fast trot to catch up with Harold as soon as possible. Waves of swords, spears and pitchforks stab at the sky at a run, as if the very clouds are the enemies they taunt.

"Now we have no choice but to chase William back to a battleground of his own choosing," laments Harold. "Which will likely be the very hill I chose myself."

Some hours later his prediction proves to be the case and they find themselves at the bottom of the slope they had intended to command.

Gyrth and Leofwyne have rejoined Harold's men and they set up camp where Harold had originally intended William to be. It is late afternoon and the weak January sun is already sunk low over the horizon. It is bitterly cold, but Harold's heart burns with a passionate fire.

This is his moment.

DEATH'S DOMINION

At first light the next day Ludec emerges from his tent to see the battle lines already drawn. There is a pervasive, strange silence as if the whole world is waiting for something magnificent, excitedly anticipating a moment of immense significance.

Ludec's first thoughts, as always, are for Astrid and their baby, due any day now. He stretches as he surveys the splendid rows of fluttering pennants, marking both their front lines and those of the enemy high on the hill.

He involuntarily gasps as he notices for the first time the solid wall of heavy horses stretching from one side of the hilltop to the other. It is a sight that clutches at the heart; colourfully bedecked horses snorting in the morning chill, their breath turning to clouds of vaporous mist. Impenetrable, formidable, and yet at the same time seemingly supernatural and ephemeral.

He knows that behind the cavalry, still thousands strong, impatiently wait the heavily armoured infantrymen and behind them, ranks and ranks of archers. It will be the archers from whom they will first hear, a soft hum that will fill the heavens but which will rain down hellfire.

Ludec studies his own front lines of infantrymen, most of them dressed more for a day's ploughing than the battlefield. Yet still their own flags fly proud and he can sense the confidence and determination of these Englishmen. Yes, they stand every chance of victory this day.

Just at the very moment that he wonders why he himself has not been woken for battle he spies the King in full battle armour, trotting towards him on his horse, his Lady Edith at his side. She looks resplendent in light armour over a flowing, white garb.

"Ah, so you awaken at last," smiles the King, without rancour. "You see I allow my chief advisers the benefit of extra sleep to keep their brain clear. But now you must take to the line. Orfur will show you the Royal Armoury – feel free to choose any weapon that suits.

"I particularly recommend the large shields. The arrows will come soon and you may thank me for that advice."

LUDEC

The King is in fine humour. He knows victory is within his grasp. Ludec spots Orfur waiting patiently for his attention and, after a polite bow to the King and his Lady, follows him into a silk pavilion stacked with racks of weapons.

He whistles through his teeth as he surveys swords of all breadths and lengths, bows and maces.

"I don't understand... " he starts. "If all this is available, why are many of our men facing the Normans with hammers and scythes?"

Orfur shrugs resignedly. "They choose to fight with whatever they are most comfortable with. If you face your final hour, you don't want to start experimenting with how well a new sword sits in your heft."

Ludec had to admit he saw some logic in this but nonetheless picks for himself a lethal and varied arsenal of weapons, including a two-handed broadsword.

He sees Orfur's curious expression.

"The rest I will keep at my feet," he grins but the humourless Master-at-Arms doesn't respond.

Outside Orfur 'advises' him to stand at the rear of the infantry lines. "King's orders," he explains.

Ludec stands his ground, jostling for position, and places his huge shield alongside his bow and quiver, and a smaller, lighter sword. He stuffs a slim misericord dagger inside his belt. His comrades-in-arms look at him quizzically, compelling him to say something in response. He knows that since he has been 'promoted' to the King's court he has been a stranger to the men.

"There's a spare shield in my tent if anyone wants it," he smiles. "This Big Bertha is the one for me."

"No thanks," grins a friendly enough face. "Plenty of room for us all under there when the arrows come."

Ludec remembers well from Stamford Bridge that these tense minutes before battle are filled with humorous quips. It is the way many men face their demons. Fear quelled, but not of course conquered, by humour. But then comes the moment when the jokes have to stop. They had all been waiting for it and here it was – an almost deafening swish and a hum that soothed as much as it petrified.

DEATH'S DOMINION

"COVER!" barks the unnecessary command up and down the lines and the drone is all but drowned out by the rush to to get under their shields, seeking shelter from the slender slivers of death.. Like the Romans centuries before them, the English ranks metamorphasise into a giant turtle back. The clang of steel tip on metal and the thud on wood reverberates through the early morning, thousands of tiny hammers striking at an anvil.

Ludec hears screams from victims but surprisingly few, their very rarity making them all the more pitiful; lone cries in the wilderness.

"ARCHERS!" is screamed along the English ranks and those same sounds of battle are reversed. Thousands of longbows pulled taut and then released, then the humming that stills the heart and the final clatter as arrows strike metal and wood. Again, the occasional scream from atop the hill sounds more like a mistake. Someone not paying attention.

This tit for tat continues for an hour, and Ludec knows it is one of the least dangerous aspects of the battle.

It is the lone, renegade arrow that kills more effectively. He considers this blanket overshoot almost as predictable as the rules of a well-marshalled game. They shoot, we take cover; we shoot, they take cover, he thinks to himself. Any man felled thus simply had his mind on something else.

But that first hour finally comes to an end and brings upon them the moment every Englishmen secretly fears. This time the noise is different: like a thunder that starts evenly enough in the distance, and then grows to a roar that sounds like Armageddon itself: the very ground vibrates under the charge of the heavy horses that becomes an earthquake threatening to swallow everything whole.

"PIKES!" goes the order up and down the line. But the arrows continue to fly and this time the pikemen in the front are at the mercy of the monstrous shadow that periodically eclipses the hazy sun.

The thundering of hooves gets louder and louder as the mighty war horses trundle over the grass down, down, down and closer and closer to the quaking English lines.

"HOLD STEADY!"

And miraculously Ludec sees the first wave of cavalry stopped in its tracks by the solid wall of lowered pikes. The horses – trained not to balk – simply cannot penetrate the line and rear up threatening to send their heavily armoured knights sprawling to the ground.

This is Ludec's first time facing heavy horses in battle, as it is for most of the army, and he draws sharp breath in relief that they can be held back. The chaos from fallen or rearing horses prevents further attacks from waves of cavalry following behind, and all along the line men and beast beat a tactical retreat.

As they flee, unprotected, back up the hill they are vulnerable to volleys of English arrows. The English ranks screech with delight at the sight of scores of Norman knights plunging from their saddles, already dead before they hit the grass.

One knight, unhorsed just yards away, stands his ground and bravely faces the English line, his sword raised threateningly at his side. It takes just a short thrust for the three nearest pikemen to pierce his chain mail which spurts red on silver. He slumps, surprised, to his knees and then forward onto his face.

"Merde!"

Ludec, along with comrades either side of him, has so far done nothing useful in this battle, save protect his own skin when the arrows fly. But now the line of pikes three rows in front of him is visibly thinning and he can see the Normans could possibly thrust through if they detected a weak spot. He is shaking but not ashamed. He is not alone.

The day wears on and hours later Ludec gets his first chance at real combat when the dissolving lines before him cry out to be bolstered. He edges forward between two other swordsmen. Abandoned pikes lie before them on the ground, a bequeath.

William has changed tactics. He is losing too many horses, his favoured and most feared weapon. Ludec can see the Norman cavalry being kept in reserve for the time being, either side of the battlefield. The infantry advance.

Ludec hears the cry go up from on top of the hill even above the screams and yells of the amassed battle hordes. He watches almost in disbelief as the Norman foot soldiers begin to march down the hill; straight at him. This time he is in the front line.

English archers take down dozens and dozens in the inexorable advance, but still they come on, hardly seeming to notice the bodies of their fallen comrades. Ludec knows that in just minutes from now he will be fighting hand to hand, yet his quaking stops. His limbs are still and battle readied. He is breathing evenly.

Now the Normans are upon them and it is sword upon sword as men scream to boost their courage and cut, slash and thrust in close combat. Ludec is hardly aware which cries are his own as he takes down one, then two, three Normans with his flailing broadsword, brandished above his head like some demon.

He steps forward of the line to give his threshing death dealer more room for manoeuvre and stabs and slashes faster than he can think. If he thinks, he will die.

A gash appears on his left arm, a smear of red blood, but he continues to wield his broadsword around his head.

"Astrid!" he screams. "Astrid!" and plunges ever deeper into the fiercely fighting Norman line. He is aware only that he is finding it more and more difficult to keep his balance in the growing pile of bodies all around.

He mustn't think, just cut and thrust. Suddenly his sword sinks into the soft unprotected chest of a foot soldier who shrieks in pain and clutches the blade with bloodied hands. The shriek surprises Ludec and he can't understand why the falling soldier won't let go – he appears to be pulling the blade deeper to him.

It is a near fatal lapse. Ludec almost seems to be on the point of dropping his sword and cradling the dying soldier in his arms when a gauntleted hand grabs him by the uninjured shoulder. He turns to face his attacker and sees Etheld, his right hand parrying a blow from a Norman swordsman while his left yanks Ludec back towards the English front line. The action wakes Ludec from his stupor and he stumbles back to his place where, his broadsword abandoned, he picks up the smaller blade.

He turns immediately and rushes back to Etheld's side. He is vaguely aware that the Norman soldier is still on his knees, still alive, and still tightly clutching the blade of Ludec's broadsword. Ludec yells a guttural curse as he thrusts his sword at the soldier's heart, ending his pitiful misery.

"AAAAASSSTTRRRRRRIIIIID!!!!" he screams at the top of his voice and continues his furious fight at Etheld's side.

In a tiny cottage on the Isle of Wit, a newborn baby also cries, passionately giving vent to her lungs just as her father is doing at that very moment. It is a sound to give life dominion over death. Claude is also there in the room, a stupid grin on his face, as his friend the ship's healing woman holds the bloodied infant high for Astrid to see.

"Sky," whispers Astrid as she stares with unbounded love at the baby's piercing blue eyes. "Come home, Ludec, and meet Sky, your baby daughter. Delivered by a Norman."

"Ciel?" muses Claude, amused. "Hmmm. Très bien."

* * * * *

It is three o'clock. The battle has raged for seven long hours. The weak sun is already sinking.

Harold has stood his ground against wave after wave of Norman attack, from cavalry and infantry.

"Sire, you have not once given the order to advance," observes Etheld during a short lull. "You are content to let William exhaust himself?"

Ludec is nearby and overhears the conversation, a hurried bandage stained with blood wrapped around his left arm.

"Many times our men appeared to waver," the King replies. "But each time we are reinforced by our flanks. Our strength lies in our sheer weight of numbers. If we reverse the situation and advance up the hill, it will be our bodies that are piled like slaughtered cattle.

"William's only way out is down. But we have to do nothing. If William wants to feed his men he will soon have to slaughter his own horses. We... " he indicates a supply line that is bringing in food even as the battle rages, "... we can survive here for months."

Harold beckons Ludec over and puts a paternal arm around his shoulders.

"Did you see this young fellow do battle this day?"

Etheld smiles. "He was a demon, sire. I counted twelve bodies at his feet."

"And you saved my life when I lost my broadsword... " Ludec hastily points out, embarrassed.

"And you mine!" adds Etheld generously.

All three men stare up the hill, wondering at the break in the fighting.

"I wonder what he is doing now," reflects Ludec.

"Preparing to cook up a nag or two to feed his men, I shouldn't wonder," grins Harold.

* * * * *

It is nearly dusk. The frost once more begins to bite. William launches his last-ditch charge. He knows that if he can break through the English lines he can turn and fight on two fronts. It is a desperate strategy but the only one left open to him.

"This thing shall end today," he mumbles to himself, and those around him strain to hear, eager to catch any whisper of command that will turn their despair to victory.

"We shall not spend another night on this English molehill nursing our wounds."

He lets his archers pour more terror upon the troops below for the last half hour of daylight and then before complete darkness falls he gives the order to charge as loud as his voice will carry.

The ground trembles under the pounding weight of several thousand hooves.

"Mort ou Gloire!" he screams, his voice croaking with fatigue, cold and emotion.

CHAPTER FOUR

THE AFTERMATH: A SECRET REVEALED

Tho' This Ingot Can'st Be Weigh'd...

William's dreams for the English throne lie crushed underfoot like the midwinter grass as he gallops downhill to his inevitable doom. His hopes and lofty ambitions, which burn so fiercely in his heart, will soon lay as cold as his body at the foot of a frosty slope.

Bewildered, mesmerised, Ludec watches the Duke's insane charge ahead of his troops. The desperate Duke's sword flails madly over his head. He is swept to his death by the snorting, nightmare demon that is his armoured steed.

The end is quick.

Acting as one, six pikemen ignore orders and step forward to meet him. William's sword almost cleanly severs the head of one and then a second before clattering to the ground, knocked from his grasp by the sea of spikes. His gauntleted hands clasp a third pikeman by the neck in a loving, solemn embrace, pulling him slowly but strongly onto the long, ugly spikes of his war saddle.

Ludec winces at the shrill scream of the pikeman, his eyes just bloody sockets married forever to the Duke's horse, carried off still screaming and convulsing horribly as the frightened steed first rears and then gallops away without his rider, but with a new passenger.

William is on his back on the grass, a broken pike through his left thigh. Ludec, just 20 feet away, is impressed by the calm expression on his face as his visor is thrown clear. He seems deep in thought, almost amused. There are more intolerably loud shouts as excited English infantrymen bolt their way through their own pikemen to get at the fallen Duke, plunging eager blades deep into his chest and heart. It is over. As if a drum or horn has sounded a pre-arranged signal, the battlefield becomes suddenly still and hushed.

In the gloom Ludec surveys the Norman front-line cavalry, some 30 feet behind the Duke, shivering to a chaotic halt. For the first time that diabolic day he can hear a bird singing. A nightjar is greeting the deepening dusk.

"They don't know what to do," a pikeman whispers to Ludec. All eyes are fixed on the becalmed Norman lines part-way down the hill.

"It is hopeless. They must surrender," mutters Etheld to Ludec's right. "We are still well over 14,000 strong. They must be down by half at least."

Harold ushers his horse through his own front lines to stand a moment beside William's body. He looks down almost reverently and crosses himself. Then he lifts his gaze to the Normans. In the uncanny silence he yells, his voice clear and strong: "Lay down your arms. Let there be no more bloodshed."

"Sire! Sire! Come back," calls Etheld. "Come back behind your men."

But the King ignores him and the shuffling fetlocks of his impatient stallion seem to be the only movement in the entire world.

Then there is a noise, which grows and grows, as one by one the Normans throw down their weapons. The clatter of the remaining 4,000 swords and shields grows to a crescendo as loud as the earlier bedlam of battle.

A single cheer goes up from the English lines, followed by another and another until the entire army is chanting and singing in delight.

As darkness falls, King Harold officially accepts the surrender of the remnants of William's invaders and impulsively deigns to be merciful, magnanimous in victory. The defeated army spends the night at its own camp on the hill, relieved of all weapons. Harold's men similarly stay put at the bottom, and guards are posted around the perimeter.

The next day the King orders the prisoners to give the dead of both sides a Christian enough burial in giant pits each containing 100 bodies.

"You fought like the mighty warrior you are," Harold tells Ludec. "Your lady can be proud of you. I am proud of you. England is proud of you." They are standing on the slope that will henceforth be known as Harold's Hill. Where just hours ago it was a scene of desperate savagery, it now stands silent and respectful.

Ludec begs the King to let him now travel to the Isle of Wit to see his wife but Harold is reluctant.

"Let us wait until we hear more about the situation," he says. "It may pass that I shall have to send a force to quell the Norman survivors there."

It is the King's turn to offer counsel.

"Meanwhile I can't have my most trusted adviser running straight into a trap, now can I, Sir Ludec?" Harold turns to allow Etheld and others around them to appreciate the joke. Their mild and respectful chuckling perplexes Ludec.

He is slow to catch on but, shocked, finally drops to one knee before his King.

"Sire, I know not what to say."

Harold draws his sword and the assembled court claps genteelly as he touches Ludec first on the right and then the left shoulder. His wound there still pains him but he hides the smarting in his eyes.

"Say nothing, Sir Ludec, for you have already said enough to save England," continues the King, his tone grave and imperious. "Without your admirable advice, England would be under the yoke of the Norman usurper. I was too hasty. You counselled me well. "

Later at dinner in the Royal Pavilion, Harold continues to sing his young friend's praises and to stress before everyone his gratitude for his timely advice.

"And you had the good sense to listen, like a true monarch," adds a voice from lower down the table. The King turns his way and blinks his eyes slowly in appreciation. His right hand offers up a small regal wave and he gives a slight nod.

THE AFTERMATH: A SECRET REVEALED

Ludec raises his eyes to his. "But, sire, I beg you. Let me travel to assure my wife's safety. You know she is with child and I fear for her life with the shipwrecked Normans on the Isle of Wit."

"We will be marching that way soon enough," insists the King. "There are things I must attend to in Winchester for I have a campaign, a dream, in which you will surely play your part. But first we must hasten to London to give thanks in proper fashion. For this I want you by my side. THEN you may proceed to your lady and mayhap even be present at the birth. I trust you shall call the child Harold?"

Ludec, deeply disappointed, lowers his head to hide his thoughts, and secretly wonders how Astrid would feel about that. It is a dilemma he doesn't even want to think about. Besides, God willing, it may not even be a boy.

The next few weeks drag agonisingly slowly for Ludec but he sticks like glue to the King's side during the march to London where the victory celebrations run riot for three days.

Messengers bring news that he now has a baby daughter called Sky and that the surviving Normans on the island are not considered a threat. Reports filter back that in defeat, they have adopted an entirely peaceful stance and at any rate number less than 200.

In Westminster Abbey, Harold delivers a series of stirring speeches concerning a return to times of Arthurian grace and announces his intention to wreak further vengeance on the Danes. Even notwithstanding Duke William's brutality, he can never forget the centuries of harassment the Vikings had inflicted and the blood they had shed on his shores.

One night over supper in the abbey, the King has good news for Ludec, who marvels at the giant tapestries hung on the stone walls behind them. But the minions and lackeys who wait on their King's every command make him a little uncomfortable.

"Tomorrow we start for Winchester where I shall unravel more of my ideas," he tells Ludec and Etheld, whom he has also knighted, as Lady Edith sits silently by, smiling graciously.

Addressing Ludec, she adopts a mysterious, confidential tone: "You will have some wonderful news to impart to your Lady Astrid," she promises. "Truly wonderful. Exciting too – for both of you."

"For all THREE of you," the King gently reminds, placing his hand lovingly over hers and fixing Ludec with a benevolent, almost fatherly gaze.

"And I hear that you failed to fulfil my wish to have your daughter named after your King," he jokes. "Did Lady Astrid object, do you suppose?" There is good-natured laughter along the table and deep down inside Ludec finds himself deeply relieved that his child has been born a girl.

The King waves away a servant's polite offer to pour him more wine and turns conspiratorially to Etheld who leans towards him, smiling enigmatically.

"On our journey tomorrow we shall travel first to Glastonbury. I have something there I wish to show young Sir Ludec."

"Indeed you have, sire," agrees Sir Etheld. "Indeed you have."

If Ludec overhears, he doesn't show it. He is too excited by the prospect of finally journeying to the south-west. He will be inching ever nearer to those closest to his heart – his real queen and princess.

* * * * *

"There – climb down," the King is clearly excited, almost like a child at Christmas. Ludec has never seen him like this.

The two stand there with Etheld outside a half-open wooden door deep in the basement of Glastonbury Abbey.

"Surely we can go no further down?" says Ludec. "We must be deep in the bowels already!"

"Indeed we are," smiles Etheld and Ludec can't help notice that he too looks like the cat that got the cream. What is it with these two?

He studies the powerfully built door and marvels at the massive hinges and locks that adorn it. Beautiful it may have been, yet this door – thick as a man's thigh – wasn't constructed to look pretty. This door, Ludec considers, is here to keep something in – or something out.

Harold's gentle pat on his upper back encourages him to take the offered torch and descend into the darkness. The stone stairs spiral steeply and there is room for only one at a time.

THE AFTERMATH: A SECRET REVEALED

"Have a care," urges Etheld as the three of them pick their way downward, the King in the middle.

It seems to take an age to reach the bottom, their steps ringing and echoing eerily off the steep, damp walls, but finally they stand on a straw covered floor.

"Is this a dungeon?" ponders Ludec. "Am I to meet my fate?"

"Perhaps it would have been wise to name your daughter as requested," whispers Harold and Ludec turns to face him to make sure he is jesting. Ludec tries to grin back, uncertainly.

"Observe this key," adds Harold, holding up the ornately decorated length of iron they had used to gain entry. "It was made by the finest locksmith in the land. There can be no copy."

Etheld is anxious to join in. "It is not forged to lock people away," he says, enjoying the mystery he is creating. "It is a special key designed to keep something safe; something very, very special."

The King now takes the lead and strides purposefully to the far side of the hall in which they stand. There is another door, much like the first, but with a much less grand lock. Harold takes a smaller key from under the folds of his blue, ermine-trimmed gown.

It creaks open. Etheld steps quickly inside and efficiently tours the circumference of the round room, lighting a series of torches on the walls with his own. This room is strangely cool and dry, with a distinct breath of fresh air coming mysteriously from somewhere. A natural duct, thinks Ludec.

His eyes nearly pop with wonder. In the centre of the room stands a solid stone table, itself encrusted with jewels and calligraphed with filigree gold-leaf lettering. There are words in Latin that he recognises, but only a few - Rex, Pax - their sigils alive with colour.

But it is what is on top of the table that threatens to steal his very breath. Jewels and caskets, gold crucifixes and crowns, silver belts buckled with precious stones of every hue. There are swords and daggers that were never meant to draw blood; simply to dazzle the beholder with their magnificence.

"The crown jewels," mutters Ludec, his mouth agape. "I thought these were kept at Westminster Abbey. I have never seen anything like it."

"No, not the crown jewels," confides Harold, waving a gently admonishing finger at Ludec as Etheld chuckles quietly beside him. "Not exactly."

"Then... what?" Ludec is too overcome to think and he wonders why he has been shown this place.

"The history is unclear," Harold continues. "But these artefacts have been handed down for three or four centuries, from royal house to royal house. They are originally believed to have been of the court of Pendragon and imbued with sorcerer's magic."

He stays silent a moment, allowing this information to sink into his young friend's dazzled brain.

"Magic?" It is all Ludec can manage and Harold turns away dismissively, at once scoffing at the very idea.

"It is all legend – folklore and legend," he goes on. "We have never detected any magical properties. We don't, for instance, believe that any of these swords is the fabled Excalibur, wondrous though they are."

Again he pauses before continuing: "The bards seem vague about the Arthurian stories. Tales of knights and damsels in distress may all be just that, tales. But these glittering tokens... " he waves his arm expansively around the room, ".... are believed to have been passed down from those mystical times."

"Various inscriptions we have deciphered instruct that the very existence of these treasures should remain the secret of kings," breaks in Etheld. "The treasure you see before you now has been passed down, sovereign to sovereign, for many generations. It is priceless – yet it is worthless, because the monarchs of England each swear an oath NEVER to sell any part of it."

The King's soft but cynical laugh interrupts Etheld's flow. "No matter how tempting that prospect might be."

Ludec goes to the table and gestures for permission to touch the goblets and chalices laying there. The King grants him leave with a wave of his arm and Ludec picks up a long sword encrusted with jewels. He handles it as he might a baby, as if at any moment it might start to wail.

"But no Excalibur?" he asks, disappointed. Etheld and Harold sadly shake their heads. "And no magic?"

THE AFTERMATH: A SECRET REVEALED

"I'm afraid not," says Harold and he and Etheld exchange a mysterious, almost playful glance. "Except... "

"Yes?" says Ludec, impatient at their games.

"Take a look at that casket in the centre, behind the three silver bowls."

Ludec locates the casket and admires its glittering glory. Haltingly, he reads an old English inscription on the front out loud.

"'Tho'... this ingot can'st be weigh'd... from its heart all things are made.' What does that mean?"

"We've no idea. Take a look inside. Go ahead." The King is beside himself now, as eager as a child around the Christmas tree.

Gingerly Ludec opens the casket lid. There is no lock, but it is heavy. He can't hide his disappointment.

"It's empty!" He stares at the green velvet plinth that presumably once displayed some ring or trinket. "Whatever it was has gone."

"An ingot," explains the King. "It's an ingot."

"An ingot that has taken its leave," insists Ludec, closing the lid and opening it again, this time looking for hidden compartments.

"Has it?" The King and Etheld are still enjoying some great mystery. Ludec hopes he is about to be enlightened. He studies the casket closer still, gently prodding at the velvet. There is a small imprint where the ingot once sat.

"I can see where it was, but it most certainly isn't there now," he insists.

"Would it surprise you if I told you the ingot is sitting there, staring at you?" The King is clearly enjoying himself. For the first time Ludec dares to wonder at his sanity. Etheld's too.

"Yes, it would," he replies simply, but continues to study the velvet plinth, his face so close he can almost feel its texture on his cheek.

"I thought the same, once," adds Harold. "But the stark truth is that every now and then the ingot becomes visible. Run your finger over the depression in the velvet – you won't feel a thing. But it's there. I've seen it."

Ludec now has serious doubts about his King's sanity. Did I offer up my life to fight for a madman, he asks himself. But his face betrays nothing.

"You don't believe me and I don't blame you," says the King sadly, resigned. "Etheld has seen it too." Behind him Etheld nods vigorously.

"Three times I have seen it," adds Etheld. "First a shimmering, as if something is somehow struggling to be there. Then, as I watched, it metamorphosised into a solid, dark object, a black ingot. Blacker than you have ever seen."

"What is it?" Ludec finds the stirrings of belief in his heart. These two men, who stood beside him in battle just days ago, are not insane. He knows he can trust them. Really trust them both. And if they say a mysterious ingot disappears and then reappears...

He shakes his head in disbelief. "What is it?" he repeats. He can think of nothing else to say.

"Nobody knows," owns the King. "It is made of a material beyond our understanding. The most trusted royal alchemists over the centuries have tried to study it. But it appears haphazardly and only for a very short time. Perhaps two minutes is the longest I have ever seen it.

"Then it may vanish again for weeks, months. Nobody has any idea what it is made of, but the legend says it comes from Merlin's cave."

"There are no writings, but the legend is that it is made of something called Dark Matter," interjects Etheld. "But what that is and where that rumour was born is utter mystery."

Ludec is stunned into silence. He rubs his chin as he stares at the centre of the velvet plinth, willing it to show itself to him.

"You will witness it, one day," promises Harold. "But, apart from that, it does us no good. It doesn't tell us the future or bring us good luck. It is, as well as most often invisible, totally inert."

"Perhaps, years from now greater minds than ours will discover its secrets," predicts Etheld. "But until then, the Dark Matter ingot remains a precious enigma."

The three men look at each other a long moment. Then Harold shivers. "It is cold down here. Come, let us return to the surface and supper. We have a long ride west on the morrow."

As they leave, Ludec hesitates in the doorway, again trying to will the ingot to reveal itself to him in the light of his waning torch. He imagines, or thinks he imagines, a faint shimmering as the other men had described. But before he can be sure, the huge door closes behind him with a massive clang that echoes through the dark underground corridors.

Later in the abbey's great hall, servants are waiting for the King's command.

"I have no need to remind you that these matters are for our ears only," says Harold gravely. "The ingot tells us not the future yet I suspect the future lies therein. And it is a future in which you will have your part."

"Dark matter!" muses Ludec, rubbing his chin. "Dare I say, it sounds a little... Satanic."

"At present we have no idea," replies Etheld. "We don't actually 'sense' any evil in it... "

"Just a little... foreboding," adds Harold, putting his finger to his lips to remind them to be discreet. "But remember, this is not a secret we would ever want to get out. There is no telling what horrors might be unleashed should its existence become public knowledge."

* * * * *

Outside under the dark mantle of midnight two men are talking in hushed whispers near the stables. One sits astride a black, gently whinnying mount, whose front hoof from time to time scrapes impatiently on the cobbles. The rider leans attentively down towards the other, listening to every word. The second man, standing beside him, is Orfur, Master-at-Arms, his face set as hard as steel as he proffers up a heavy pouch of coin.

"Go!" he urges quietly, slapping the horse's rear flank with his hand and watching as the stallion melts gratefully into the night. "Go with speed."

There is a wintry chill in the grounds of the castle. But Orfur is warmed by the passion of his hatred for Ludec. It isn't simply because of the young upstart's meteoric rise to fortune and acclaim, but because he suspects the King has rewarded him with the mystery nugget to present to his wife, a gift from a grateful nation.

LUDEC

Orfur doesn't know exactly what the nugget is, but he hasn't spent nearly a year around the court without hearing rumour of its status and potential value.

And he watched covertly when the King presented Ludec with a small, silver casket earlier that day, after their mysterious visit to the inner caves under the castle.

"I may have a reward of my own for that sniveller," he scowls softly to himself under his breath.

CHAPTER FIVE

ASSASSINS

A Royal Proclamation
Let it Be Knowne that By Royal Decree His Royal Majesty King Harold the Mighty, Despoiler of Despots, announces that from this day hence England shall reclaim the title of its Fathers, ALBION and that its new Capital shall be Winchester wherein shall abide The Restored Round Table and all the King's Knights. Furthermore, the brave town of Hastings in Sussex shall from this day forth be known as ROYAL HASTINGS and let every man who shall tread its streets ever remember the Glory of January 2nd, 1067 and Give Thanks to God. Long Live The King!

While Harold delights Winchester with his plans for a noble castle and cathedral to be built there, as befits Albion's new capital, Ludec is despatched with five riders to the Isle of Wit to be reunited at last with his family.

The King is satisfied by reports that indicate there will be no trouble from the shipwrecked Normans and the patrol is deemed sufficient. Nevertheless, he sends Orfur along with a special brief to keep a watchful eye on the nation's young hero.

After disembarking from the ship at Rhydde, they travel overland by horse through thick woodland. Orfur is strangely silent and Ludec begins to believe that his elevation to knight has at last cowed the man's bitter tongue. However, he knows Orfur has the King's trust and so is content to have him along as his 'protector', although the role lends little to his ability in conversation. Every command to his four cavalrymen is a bark and beyond that he says little.

LUDEC

Ludec finds himself confiding instead in Gellick, a rider picked for his knowledge of the island.

"You lived here once, I believe," says Ludec as they trot leisurely through beech and ash, the ground dappled with the earliest signs of spring, brave sprinklings of crocuses and snowdrops.

"Aye, Sir Ludec, indeed I did. And a fair isle it is, too. Close enough to the mainland for provision, far enough for a little peace."

Ludec laughs: "You prefer island life, then?"

Gellick waves a hand good naturedly at the sweep of purples, yellows and whites at the side of the track.

"Let us say I prefer petals to politics," he smiles.

"Somebody has to involve themselves in the real world." It was Orfur, angry, brash. "Gazing at a pretty bank of snowdrops won't parry an invader's sword."

Ludec and Gellick are surprised at Orfur's vehemence.

"I believe Gellick was there on January 2nd. And in September at Stamford Bridge, Orfur. Nobody would say he was found wanting."

"I'm just saying, that's all," persists the Master-at-Arms. "Daydreaming about flowers and hiding away on an island wouldn't have kept the Normans or the Vikings at bay."

Furious, he wheels his horse around and trots to the back, ostensibly to bring up the vanguard. Ludec and Gellick exchange a glance each raising an eyebrow, taking great care that Orfur doesn't notice. When they are alone at the head of the patrol, Gellick humbly takes Orfur's part with a concession.

"It's true that sometimes Englishmen everywhere have to stand up and be counted, no matter in what paradise they may abide."

"You knew your place and stood it well," Ludec assures him. "I'm afraid the Master-at-Arms is a bitter man. He doesn't much like me."

Gellick flicks his reins gently against his mare's face as she flinches at a scampering red squirrel. "He's right that if everyone felt that way about staying out of politics, William would today be rewriting England in his own image. He would purge the very Englishness out of us: customs, politics, every little aspect of our way of life."

"But he didn't and so he won't," Ludec adds. "Whatever horrors may have awaited us under a Norman tyrant no longer concern us.

England can thrive and prosper as it has always has – and all because you for one didn't hide away on your idyllic little island."

"Albion!" calls Orfur from the rear. "It's not England any more, it's Albion."

Again Ludec and Gellick exchange a glance. Orfur had heard every word.

Some hours before dusk Ludec suggests they find an inn or a place to camp for although it is but a short way to go, he would prefer not to arrive at night. Better to rest and arrive fresh in the morning without alarming anyone. Orfur says nothing but to everyone's surprise, suddenly complains he has dropped his gauntlet and must retrace his steps a little way to find it.

As he wheels his horse and gallops back the way they have come, Ludec feels a chill of suspicion. He looks deeply into the faces of the riders at his side wondering whether, with the exception of Gellick in whom he instinctively trusts, he is riding with friend or foe.

But he senses their answer straightaway as they each draw their swords – not against Ludec but in readiness. They too smell a rat. Their horses become agitated, snorting in the cold, late afternoon mist. They too are anticipating danger.

Suddenly a loud shout fills the air and the riders just have time to detect the unmistakeable French accent in "Attaque!" before they are beset.

"Ambush!" yells Gellick and the English riders rally round Ludec in a defensive ring. Impatient and impetutous, Ludec surges forward on his horse, his sword raised challengingly above his head.

"I am not some child to be protected," he shouts and together they join in close combat with one dozen Norman knights who plunge screaming from the trees at full gallop.

But, despite their number, the attackers are no match for the courage and skill of their battle-hardened adversaries and after 20 minutes of fierce fighting, the Albion patrol is victorious. Ludec, who has been unhorsed, and now bears a large, ugly gash above his right eye, stands over three bodies he himself has slain.

"Orfur betrayed us," says Gellick quietly but sombrely. He checks the dead body of one of their own, Edik, for a pulse. Sadly, he shakes his head.

"He planned this ambush with the Norman survivors," says another. "I hope he paid them well for the cost must be higher than they expected."

"These aren't Normans," says Ludec, now kneeling at the head of a dead ambusher lying prostrate without his helmet. "Look at his shorn hair. Cut Norman style, undoubtedly, but his neck is as white as a baby's bottom. The razor must still be warm from this snip."

They check the other bodies to find the same evidence. "Neither are these Norman mounts," verifies Gellick, holding the bridle of one and stroking his long, brown face to calm him. "Local stock, I'd recognise them anywhere. They want Harold to think it was the Normans who were washed up on the island shores. And that's just what Orfur is hurrying to the King's side to tell him now. But why would he want to kill you, Sir Ludec?"

"I believe the man bears some sort of grudge against me," he replies. "But why, I have no idea. I can hardly believe he wants me dead – but if he does you can be sure he hasn't just ridden off without verifying the evidence of my demise... "

They all lift their eyes to the woods in the direction Orfur had taken and are aware of movement in the trees. They can't see his face, but they can just make out a rider in the distance, mounting his horse and galloping away to the north.

"Traitor!" calls Gellick after him, raising his fist in fury. Then turning to the others he says: "We must split up. We have lost Edik in battle but we are still four. You two return at once to Winchester – it will take at least two to convince the King of Orfur's lies."

"No," says Ludec. "I'll be safe enough now. You three go back together in case Orfur dreams up some further ugly surprises for you before you get there. Take this letter to the King... "

He strides to his horse and rummages through his saddlebag. Each man is clearly impressed when he takes out an elegant silver casket. Inside are quill, ink and parchment with which he commences to write.

"Well, you are a learned knight," grins Gellick. "And such a fine writing case."

"A gift from the King," says Ludec, concentrating.

After a moment or two Ludec waves the parchment in the air to dry the ink and then folds it before handing it to Gellick. "Take this. It will explain everything to the King to combat all the lies Orfur is bound to invent against you. It has my signature so the King shall know the truth. I will press on alone tonight with the directions I have learned from you, Gellick. A father and husband arriving alone at night will alarm no one. Now... go!"

But Ludec doesn't continue his journey very far that day. Within an hour he happens upon an inn where he gratefully takes a meal, a tankard of mead and a room for the night.

* * * * *

The first sight Ludec has of his baby daughter is something of a shock. She is being held tenderly in the arms of a Norman knight, nestling cosily against the same sort of cold chain mail that only a few weeks before Ludec had been desperately trying to pierce with bloody intent.

Sky is murmuring contentedly as Claude gazes down into her bright blue eyes and hums the tune of a French lullaby he can barely remember. He is standing outside the cottage in weak February sunshine as Astrid and her father are stuffing fresh straw mattresses inside.

Claude looks up as the rider approaches. Ludec, knowing from Gellick's directions that this was indeed the cottage and this was, in all probability, his daughter, does his best to stay calm.

He dismounts and ties his horse to a wooden post which lists drunkenly to one side, like the rest of the fence around it. This is a cottage in need of some attention, thinks Ludec.

"A fine morning," remarks Ludec genially. "And a fine child. Yours?"

"Lady Astrid," calls Claude loudly and urgently. "Lady Astrid. Please to come out please."

Almost at once she is there in the doorway just as Ludec had pictured her a thousand times during his enforced absence. She is silent as she gazes at him without comprehension. Behind her stand her father Egbert and her cousin Beatrice.

There is absolute quiet until Astrid's brain finally convinces her to believe her eyes.

"Ludec? My God – Ludec!" She rushes to his arms hardly noticing the fine clothes in which he is now dressed. A far cry from the farmer's son who had left her months before. "At last, at last," she mumbles into his shirt sleeves through tears of sheer relief.

He holds her away from him at arm's length. "Let me look at you. This is the moment I have dreamed of for an eternity."

They stand there in a trance, thirstily drinking in the vision each had longed for since the end of the previous summer. Then they again hold each other tight, tighter than they had ever embraced before.

"You're back. You're safe," she cries. "You have a war wound over your right eye. Come inside and I'll treat it."

"But otherwise intact," he mumbles and his eyes raise to the Norman knight who stands there still, looking awkward and very sheepish.

"Oh, this is Claude," explains Astrid, clumsily dragging Ludec by the hand in his direction. "We owe him so much. So much."

"And the... baby?" asks Ludec.

"That's... that's Sky, your daughter," she adds.

"Sky and Claude appear to be closely acquainted." Ludec's tone is clipped, but Astrid knows he is only playing and is, in fact, on the verge of laughter.

Claude relaxes a shade and pouts his lips at the half-dozing infant in his arms.

"Friends, yes," he says. "Sky and me. Mon ami." Then his face is creased with sudden consternation as he adds: "Oh, I think perhaps she needs changing."

Eagerly he holds the baby out for Astrid to take. "Oh, Sky, I thought we were friends," he says and all three of them finally burst into laughter. In each case it is an explosion of relief rather than amusement, but Claude and Ludec enter the cottage as friends not enemies.

* * * * *

Orfur looks threateningly at the ship's master.

"I demand that you sail NOW – it is King's business. Disobey and you shall be hanged for treason."

The sad, fat man looks up at the much taller Orfur and sweats with fear. His chubby cheeks almost tremble as he burbles his desperate explanations.

"But sire, it is a decision beyond us all to make. We cannot sail for several hours. The tides... "

Exasperated, Orfur leads his exhausted horse away from the wooden jetty and once on the bank, mounts up again. He knows his mount is almost all in after the frantic gallop through the night.

"You have another horse?" he demands, shouting.

The scared old man considers his situation for a moment and then points nervously to a nearby hut.

"If it's King's business you had better take mine. Behind the building. But she's a valuable horse."

Without a word Orfur urges his mount the last few paces before locating the old man's steed, dismounts and re-saddles the new mare.

He gallops off towards the west, hoping to find a smaller vessel that can get him off the island before his pursuers catch up. He knows he can't just stay there and wait for them.

"Tell the King, Klig Geeson, master of The Serpent – at your service," the old man is yelling at the cloud of dust already disappearing into the distance.

Orfur isn't listening; he has other concerns of greater urgency than the old man's greedy protest. Before they left Glastonbury he had seen Ludec carefully pack the mysterious casket in his saddlebag so he knew he still had it with him, clearly to offer up to his Lady Sow.

But now he must reach Winchester to procure some explanation for the King before Ludec and his patrol return. It is a desperate plan but the only one available.

Meanwhile he tries to guess as he gallops westward to the next nearest harbour how many men are in pursuit. He is fairly sure Edik's body lay slain in the clearing; that leaves four. Wracking his brain he speculates that Ludec will probably split his small force equally which means he has sent two riders after him. But neither of them will be Ludec, of that he is sure. He is too concerned with a reunion with his Lady Sow and Brat, he snarls to himself. Orfur smiles grimly with a secret belief that this will make it easy for him to concoct a story for his King, which will at least buy him some time.

* * * * *

"You are a knight?" Astrid clasps her hands together in delighted disbelief while her father puts his arm around Ludec's shoulder to pat him with reflected pride. "Because of your bravery on the field? You promised me you would be careful and stay at the back." Her pretty face grows cross as she waves an admonishing finger at him, only half in jest.

Ludec lowers his eyes shyly to the floor.

"Well, no, actually. It was more that I encouraged the King to do exactly that; stand at the back for a while instead of rushing into battle."

"And for that they knight people?" Egbert was astounded but still clearly pleased. "Kindly tell the King I would have said exactly the same. Tell him to send me my sword by special courier."

They all laugh, happy to be reunited again at last in Beatrice's small, white stone cottage in the pleasant Isle of Wit countryside. A fire burns merrily in the hearth and all is well in their world.

Claude's leading role in the drama of Sky's birth had been explained in detail and he too is part of the family as they drink toast after toast with tankards of ale and pewter goblets of wine.

"To my knight," says Astrid, her blue eyes sparkling with unabashed admiration as she raises her goblet to her lips.

"And to my Lady... and my baby daughter, Sky, may they forever outshine each other with their beauty," replies Ludec, supping deep on his mead.

Astrid lowers the goblet from her lips with a sudden realisation. "Does this really mean I am... a genuine Lady?" Her father now transfers all his affectionate pride to his daughter and cannot restrain his tears of joy.

"A Lady, true, and more besides," says Ludec. "Here's to my princesses both. No knight could serve a nobler pair of mistresses."

Later that evening with Sky asleep in her cot the mood turns more sombre as he tells them the grimmer news of Orfur's treachery and the ambush in the forest.

He turns to Claude. "They were dressed as Norman knights but we soon saw that they were imposters. Orfur must have sent a rider ahead to bribe a band of vagabonds. Exactly why I have no idea. He seems to hate me but what would it gain him?"

Claude looks thoughtful and considers the tale he has been told. "Many Norman dead washed up on the beaches here, along with survivors," he says quietly. "Disguises easy to explain. But why? That may be a mystery although such passions are common in my land. Men kill for love so why not hate?"

Ludec finishes off his tankard with a flourish and wipes his lips on his shirt sleeve. He finds he now has more burning issues to attend to and when he catches Astrid's eye he sees he is not alone in this.

"We shall investigate further on the morrow," he says, getting to his feet. "In the meantime I just hope Gellick and his men can convince the King of Orfur's evil deeds before he manages to wriggle out of it."

"Your letter should do it," says Beatrice. "You two get a good night's sleep. Egbert and I can bed down in the barn with Claude. There is plenty of room. Methinks my Lady Astrid and her knight could use a little privacy this one night."

* * * * *

Early next morning Astrid arises softly singing to herself and, after attending to Sky, leaves the cottage to fetch in more firewood from the shed. After a tender, loving glance she allows Ludec to snooze on in sated dreams of contentment and happiness.

It is a bitterly cold morning, too infant to feel any warmth from the weak sunshine that yesterday she believed would be heralding the coming spring.

She is still humming as she takes her woven basket to the woodshed and stoops to one knee in order to select likely pieces of kindling.

She smiles to herself in gratitude to Claude. Not only had he helped bring Sky safely into this life, he is now almost a member of the family, chopping firewood and helping with all the other chores. But her smile hides a deeper secret. She suspects that her cousin Beatrice has developed a soft spot for the Frenchman's charm and wonders if her willingness to go to the barn last night had just as much to do with that.

It is dark in the woodshed, with very little light able to penetrate through the tiny, high window. Inexplicably the door creaks slowly shut behind her, blocking out the sunlight entirely. Suddenly a sharp noise puts her senses on full alert: the sound of snapping wood – but not from her.

"Who's there?" she starts but immediately her voice is cut off as a hand goes around her mouth and she feels the cold blade of a dagger against her pulsing throat. She tries to bite but the gauntlet is thick and tough.

"So you must be the Lady Sow, light of the sniveller's eye," says a voice, rough and manic in the darkness. She can already feel the warm trickle of her own blood on her neck and trembles in fear.

In what she believes to be her last thoughts, she laments that so much intense happiness should end so miserably in a dank, sullen woodshed.

CHAPTER SIX

FOR A QUILL AND A POT OF INK

"'Tis only a dig from the point of my dagger – stop your bleating. You may yet live if you answer my questions square."

Orfur's cold hostility chills Astrid to the marrow and she instinctively knows that taking her life means nothing to him. She is just a lump of warm meat between him and whatever it is he wants. She sinks to her knees, aware of the sweet smell of the damp wood piled around her and something else: a man's stale sweat and the stench of her own fear.

"Where is it?" he barks and the question surprises her. She can see nothing in the gloom.

"Where is what?" She almost chokes with the effort of speech. A broken twig is pressing into her knee, hurting her, but she dare not move.

"The casket, sow. The silver casket."

Orfur licks his lips, cherishing this moment. He knows that this trembling creature at his feet is under his total control. He can kill her, beat her, kiss her. While he holds the knife to her throat he can force her to disrobe. He can even have her. This is what he thrives on. The passion of power surges strong like a drug. For these precious seconds he is his own King, a god. Elation throbs through his veins as pure adrenaline.

She is ashamed as an uncontrollable trickle of warm urine runs down her leg. She prays he doesn't notice. The last vestige of her naked, threadbare pride can't take it.

LUDEC

"My God, wretch, have you pissed yourself?" His low brutal laugh is bestial and triumphant. "You're not fit to potty train your brat. The runt should teach you." She is so destroyed she wishes she were already dead. He bends slightly to bury his face momentarily in her soft hair and she can feel his urgent bulge against the back of her neck. She wants to be sick.

He had planned to return to Winchester, to race the remainder of the patrol back to Harold and to invent a cover story of how he had discovered Ludec secretly plotting against the King. He surely would trust his word after so many months of loyal service to the throne, and his father before him.

But he had failed to find a vessel small enough to cheat the tide and large enough to make any speed. He had watched instead from a hilltop as Gellick and his two riders approached the ship's master of The Serpent. He saw the little fat man point excitedly to the west and presently all four boarded the ship. The tide was now right but Orfur could neither join them nor challenge them. He was outnumbered. But he now knows Ludec is alone. And if he has no future in Albion – he will steal the nugget and flee to France, a rich man.

Astrid is aware she must pull herself together if she is to survive and her befuddled mind struggles desperately to deal with Orfur's bizarre question. If he wants it, then she must 'hide' it, at least mentally.

"The casket is safe in a chest in the loft," she lies. In fact it sits in full view next to Ludec's things on a chest of drawers in the mattress room. There are only two rooms, but you have to go through the larger to get to the one with the beds, where Sky also lies sleeping.

Satisfied, Orfur releases the pressure a little. He lifts his head from hers, allowing a strand of her hair to play out between his lips. The bulge in his trousers is no longer pressed up against her.

"Who is inside?"

"Ludec is awake, dealing with the baby. My father and cousin also." She piles lie upon lie. On her knees at the mercy of a deranged thug with an inexplicable obsession for a writing case, lies are her only weapon. They may be all that keep her and her family alive.

FOR A QUILL AND A POT OF INK

"Let's go and pay your sniveller a little visit before your bowels open like your bladder."

Orfur drags her roughly to her feet, his hand still over her mouth. Intensifying sunlight hurts her eyes as he bundles her outside and towards the cottage door. He stands beside it, behind her, with the dagger pressed to the small of her back. He wants there to be no doubt that its blade means business.

"Call him," he whispers. "And keep your tongue sweet or you both die. Your runt as well."

"Ludec," she calls softly.

"Louder!"

She clears her throat to raise her voice a little. "Ludec! We have a visitor."

She can feel the dagger dig a little deeper at the base of her spine, then astonishingly the pressure is suddenly released and with some surprise she feels the heavy weight at her back slump to the grass, just as Ludec appears startled before her. He is wearing nothing but his britches and is rubbing his face on a towel.

"Claude!" he gasps and Astrid turns to see Orfur's body twitching on the ground, a sickle embedded deep between his shoulder blades. His eyes are open wide like a stunned deer, and blood is oozing copiously from his back and his mouth. The Norman too is standing right behind her, glad to have got the nasty job done.

Ludec takes his wife in his arms to inspect the wound on her neck, wiping the trickle of red with his towel.

"Where the devil did he come from?"

"He wanted the silver casket," gasps Astrid. "I think he was going to butcher us all."

"What on earth does he want with the writing case?"

They stare down at Orfur, choking on his last breath.

"*Writing ca...?*" he manages in a hoarse whisper before his eyes yield and glaze and his bodily spasms finally cease. He dies with the knowledge that his mission, such as it was, has all been for a quill and a pot of ink.

"I see you found your gauntlet," Ludec whispers almost to himself, an ironic requiem.

LUDEC

Egbert and Beatrice have now appeared and are leading Astrid inside to treat her wounds, which are only slight, and Ludec is left alone with Claude.

The two men, both bare-chested in the morning cold, are silent for a moment. Ludec offers his hand which Claude eagerly takes in both his. They shake vigorously, with the warmth of brothers.

"I never thought I'd owe my life to a Norman," says Ludec with a depth of sincerity that impresses even he.

CHAPTER SEVEN
THE TRAPPINGS OF FATE

For Lady Astrid, the next few weeks are an insane dream from which she is afraid she will one morning awake. She has seen Ludec officially knighted with great ceremony by the King in Winchester, her breath coming in short gasps at the unbelievable pomp, the grand music and the feasting afterwards: all for her young husband. It is held in a large church, adjoining land where architects have already had the footings marked out for the castle and cathedral which will together give the new capital its authority and authenticity.

She visibly shakes when the smiling King himself offers her his hand. She takes it cautiously in hers and struggles desperately not to stumble as she curtseys in as ladylike a fashion as she can manage. She is surprised at his tall, powerful stature, his pleasing features and intelligent, ready wit.

"Your husband fights like a lion, but has the stealth and cunning of a fox. His youthful wisdom changed the fate of our island forever," he tells her, and she finds herself grappling to comprehend it really is Ludec he is talking about. Ludec, whose soft hands and honeyed voice had wooed her heart. Ludec, who once dropped her freshly baked cakes into the dirty wash-water by accident. Ludec, who sometimes forgets where he has left his boots. Now Ludec is not only a hero but a nobleman knight with lands gifted by his eternally grateful King.

Now she is standing by Edith Swan-neck's side, each of them as resplendent as the other in long, flowing gowns of fine linen. Edith, instinctively sensible to her youthful inexperience and shyness, happily gesturing at the long, wide pastures before them, which lead down to the most fabulous country house Astrid has ever seen.

It is a large, timber-built building with a thatched roof – as large as a manor house. But the thing that thrills her most is that it is on two storeys. She has never seen this in her life before.

"This... " Edith pauses for full effect, "is your new home. Welcome home, my Lady Astrid."

As Astrid surveys the pleasant sight spread out before her like a cake before a saucer-eyed child, Edith turns to survey her face, enjoying the sheer disbelief she sees there. She too has recently given birth to twin boys, and well knows the joy of motherhood.

The King and Sir Ludec are already walking down a wide gallery of stone steps towards the house, but Astrid is dumb-struck. She clasps her hands before her and simply looks with joy from the house to Edith and back to the house again.

"My Lady." Claude, their new chief manservant, steps forward to her side, Sky dozing dreamily in his arms. "May we enter? I think Sky would prefer to be in warmer air."

There is one, huge room almost as big as a castle's banqueting hall. Astrid looks around in every nook and cranny with an excitement fit to burst. Large tapestries hang on the walls. "Just like a castle..." Astrid finally manages to stutter. A staircase rises from the room, itself 30 strides from one end to the other, up into a gallery along which are placed four bedrooms side by side. It is of course the same space as downstairs, divided up into quarters.

Astrid takes the stairs like a newborn lamb, cooing at first this room and then that. "This is ours," she says in the first, and then "no, this is ours" in the second, and again in the third and yet again in the fourth. All have stunning views over the expanse of their pastures, walled gardens and orchards.

"You shall have a staff of two," announces Edith as they stare through one upper window at an elderly gardener tending to a bed of flowering herbs. "There is a kitchen garden which will provide you with everything you need and, of course, there are horses in the stable to fetch you to Winchester whenever you desire."

"I cannot believe my eyes. They must be playing me a cruel joke," says a delighted Astrid, as she pulls back the translucent animal skin to better see the view outside. Goats and sheep graze on the low grass. Nearby two cows and three pigs saunter lazily through a muddied paddock.

"These are the trappings of fate," smiles Edith kindly.

"Nonsense, these are the rewards of valour. The prizes of heroism," it is the King, walking into the room with Ludec.

Ludec himself is also speechless. He and Claude exchange a slight smile, conspirators in silent amazement. Unlike Astrid, Ludec feels compelled to hide his wonderment, in case it is considered unworldly.

Downstairs, Astrid runs her fingers over a pane of stained coloured glass in an adjoining small annexe that is designated a chapel. She traces the contoured relief of St Alban and holds her breath in awe. "Our own glass," she murmurs. "We have our very own glass."

Outside in the grounds, she turns to Edith to enquire about a smaller, humbler building standing off on its own.

"For the servants," she tells her.

Still in the house, the King is talking gravely with Ludec: "This used to belong to a Duke. He was discovered plotting with Harelda and the Danes before I took the throne. Edward was red-faced with fury but the Duke and his family fled before he could be arrested and executed.

"As is the custom, the house was returned to the Crown and I planned to give it to one of my new Knights of the Round Table. Gyrth and Leofwyne were first knighted and they of course are already well looked after. Then came Etheld who has a grand estate in Northampton, so I am pleased to present it to you, my fourth knight."

They can hear Edith and Astrid giggling excitedly like young girls some way off in the gardens and watch as they and Claude, still carrying the baby, head back towards the house.

"The Duke was found slain at Stamford Bridge. He had returned on the longboats hoping to reclaim his estate – with interest, no doubt! An Albion arrow was found in his eye."

A look of undisguised disgust crosses the King's handsome features. "He had his just deserts."

Thus, wide-eyed Sir Ludec and his Lady Astrid begin their new lives together cosseted with riches and comfort beyond their wildest dreams. Free Albion is a paradise they have fought for and have deservedly won. and they intend to enjoy it.

LUDEC

Ludec is allowed to stay with his family while Harold, now hailed King of Kings, outlines his plans for his new, thrusting nation. A great believer in the old Arthurian legends of chivalry and great deeds, he announces his wish for Winchester to be returned to its rightful place as Albion's capital. He vows that defeated foes the Vikings shall pay the price for their history of bloodshed.

Most of this washes over Ludec's head as he and Astrid wander hand in hand across the several acres that envelope their new home. Astrid's father and her cousin Beatrice are invited to take over a vacant farm on the outskirts of the estate, and Claude joins the manor-house staff as chief manservant. He is not the least concerned that one of his main duties is as nanny to Sky, and indeed would have been deeply disappointed had it not been so.

One day while they reconnoitre Egbert's proposed farmstead, Astrid turns to her husband with her playful, childlike charm.

"You've come a long way from feeding the pigs," she says, as they survey the empty sties and chicken shacks. "But I know you'll still want to muck in. Only now I expect you shall don gloves before filling the bucket." She is teasing but she can't hide the truth from her stunningly blue eyes, sparkling with love and with pride.

They could not have been any happier. Until late that spring when the messenger came.

They were down by the lake on a gorgeous sunny day. Sky playing happily on her back in the long grass while her parents gaze lovingly at her and each other, relaxing and stretched out with goblets of wine alongside.

A gaggle of agitated geese honk noisily, unexpectedly taking to the air and rudely disturbing the still water with broad, flapping wings. The sharp interruption is followed by a chill breeze which leaves Astrid shivering. They look up to see what has alarmed the geese and watch a sombre-looking messenger striding purposefully across the lawns from the house. Claude stands at a doorway, discreetly alert.

Somehow, some prescient horror clutches at Astrid's heart and her despair plunges deeper than the dark, reedy lake itself. This, she thinks, is surely some terrible harbinger of doom.

CHAPTER EIGHT

WHEN THE PREY SETS THE TRAP

Chase Not the Fox, Lest You Find the Wolf

"The King requests your presence," says the man all in black, sombrely. "We sail for Denmark in the summer and there are matters of import to attend in Winchester."

Ludec and Astrid have risen to their feet to greet the messenger and Ludec stares at his wife now as her blue eyes grow vacant. She doesn't seem to know where to look so she in turn is staring down at Sky, still gurgling happily on her back in the grass.

He knows that for all her professed favourable impressions of their King, his stature, wit and fairness of face, she hates him now more than anyone on earth. Ludec can read it in the deep ocean of her bright blue eyes, glazing now as if to blot out her thoughts from the world. Her dangerous thoughts, and perhaps his too at this moment, amounting to treason.

"Denmark?" asks Ludec stupidly. The messenger stays silent.

At last Astrid lifts her gaze back to him and he can see all the sorrow in the world in her stricken, dumbfounded face. "Denmark," she repeats simply and to them both it is the unholiest curse in the universe. Bells toll miserably where moments before they had chimed, skies blacken to prepare for the wrath of thunder, and as a backdrop to it all, Sky continues to chortle to a waving blade of grass, oblivious.

Ludec turns to the messenger. "When must I be in Winchester?"

"The Royal Command is that you return with me. I am to wait at your convenience."

Ludec goes, of course, as summoned. For the rest of the afternoon he and Astrid prepare his things in silence, a silence they are both afraid to break because they know it can only be followed by tears.

Finally, he is ready to take his leave, and they have to confront each other's sorrow face to face.

"I promise to stay at the back," he says weakly, holding her quaking shoulders with both hands.

"You said that before, and hid at the front."

"We'll likely be back in a month or two."

She says nothing, knowing any words will be choked by uncontrollable sobbing.

* * * * *

In Winchester, Ludec learns that Harold is planning a full-scale invasion of his own, and his advice and company is naturally required. He harbours crazy mixed emotions; he is grateful for the riches he has accrued because of his lucky intervention at Hastings, but he is a farmer not a military man.

"I am a farmer and a father," he confides to Sir Etheld. "But I'm not allowed to be either."

"Hush, boy. Your parting from Astrid is heartbreaking but you both know your new wealth and position brings with it responsibilities, unwelcome though they may be. There is simply no option. Heroes can never resign. They are heroes for life, whenever their peoples need them."

Etheld's kind old face brings comfort to Ludec. His own father died just a year ago, and he is still young enough to need an older man's experienced, steadying hand.

"And my country needs me now – or at least my King does," Ludec replies and his cynicism is safe with Etheld. They are brothers who have fought side by side and protected each other in the heat of battle: brother Knights of the Round Table.

He sees very little of Astrid and his growing daughter for the next few months while spring turns to mid-summer and mid-summer slips to embarkation day. Finally the armada is ready, and 600 ships, many abandoned on the beaches of Sussex by the Normans, and many more hewn from the great forests of Albion, especially from the nearby New Forest, set sail for the east coast where they are to rendezvous with more ships before heading for the fjords of the north.

At first the sailing is smooth, but soon enough the North Sea vents its savage fury and Ludec wonders how the Vikings ever managed to reach Albion's shores at all, let alone sail confidently to and fro decade after decade. The waves pound the ships like angry hammers and dark skies show them no mercy. Hour after hour they plough slowly northward, each ship pitching and yawing like a cork in a thunderstorm. So very, very few of them are sailors and in testimony to this, men vomit over the sides in droves, night and day.

"You're looking a little green, my friend," laughs Etheld when he finds Ludec with his arms wrapped around the foc's'le mast in a heavy, unremitting swell.

"I think he's fallen for another just as slim as his Lady," teases Gellick who has also joined them on the same ship. "If you'll pardon me observing so, Sir Ludec." They have to shout to be heard against the roar of the almost permanent storm.

Since the journey began it was clear these three were all going to be great travelling companions and Gellick was permitted to take license despite the difference in rank.

"I'm just checking these masts are set fast," rejoins Ludec. "At least I'm not helping to top up the North Sea with my insides." The three laugh as yet another soldier succumbs to the will of his stomach and stumbles to the rail to retch violently overboard.

Eventually they hear the cry they had at once both dreaded and yearned for.

"Land Ahoy!"

It takes several long hours to disembark at the tiny port of Esbjerg which has been abandoned by its few fearful inhabitants.

"Let THEM run like rabbits for a change," smirks Harold as he oversees the noisy, bustling operation of stacking mountains of supplies in the empty houses of the Viking village harbour. "Now they will smell the same fear their longboats have wrought on our people for long, long decades."

For the men it is good to be back on dry land, even if it is foreign soil. The barrels of wine and ale roll over the wooden jetties with a satisfying rumble that reminds them they have said goodbye at last to the unforgiving sea. The mood is buoyant, joyful, and even Ludec forgets his troubles for a short while.

Etheld stays on the ship and watches the busy port thronging with Albion workers. "We are 10,000 men in 600 ships – the mightiest armada that has ever sailed. We are invulnerable."

Ludec too stares at the scene but says nothing.

"Come on, let's put ashore," cries Gellick and leaps over the rail to clamber playfully along the outside of the ship to the gangplank.

"Don't fall in," warns Ludec. "These Danish seas will freeze your enthusiasm in an instant, and more besides."

Nevertheless, the three comrades make their way cheerfully into the Viking town that doesn't know it, but has already become a part of the embryonic Albion empire.

* * * * *

Days wear on into weeks, weeks wear on into months but still the killing never ceases. Settlements, villages and towns are defeated and left in flames. The Vikings have got little fight left in them since their total defeat at Stamford Bridge and eagerly join Harold's inexorable tide of victory by the hundreds, even thousands. Harold jubilantly claims the subjugated fjords and mountains for Albion's own.

By the spring of 1068, his army knows the war is unquestionably won and men allow themselves to dream of a triumphant return to their loved ones in Albion.

Another town has been sacked with hardly a Haroldian casualty and Etheld, Gellick and Ludec are relaxed around their camp fire. Smiling Viking women and children are offering the town's hospitality to this noble, conquering army. How easy merciless conquest is, muses Ludec.

WHEN THE PREY SETS THE TRAP

"Only guilt and indecision could have stopped us," says Ludec out loud and his two friends look pensive. They know his moods. "Oh that God had been pleased to send us those."

"It is only what they wanted to do to us," ventures Gellick and pipes down after a sharp look from Sir Etheld.

"It is true, Ludec," adds Etheld softly, sensing his friend's despair. "I also am a man of peace, like you. Yet I have come to realise it is either 'do or be done by'."

Etheld gestures at the happy faces all around them, fetching and carrying wine and victuals for their conquering 'heroes'. "Don't be fooled by these smiles. They would just have soon seen us sliced to pieces and our heads lofted high on spears to frighten the wolves. Perhaps Harold is right. Conquer or be conquered."

Ludec shakes his head sadly. "I am a simple man. Just a simple man. I have no wish to spend my days butchering other simple men who, like me, just want to tend their farms and cherish their women and offspring."

"You're wrong there," interrupts Gellick excitedly. "These 'simple' men here were burning our farms and ravishing and slaughtering our women while their own wives cheered heartily. Boot's on the other foot, simple as that."

Again a chiding glance from Etheld shuts him up. Sulkily he picks up bread and cheese from a wooden tray alongside his goblet of wine and lets his mouth eat instead of talk.

"You never told me how you learned to read and write." Ludec can see Etheld is determined to change the subject.

"It was my father," begins Ludec and Gellick stops his chewing for a moment to also listen to the story. "There was once a monastery of sorts about a day's ride from our farm. More of a hermitage, really. Only four or five monks... "

Ludec stares at the flames and holds his hands out to warm them. Etheld and Gellick urge him on with their silence and stillness.

"One day, when I was very small, my father was trading pelts at a market near their retreat. Prices were particularly good at that time. He was just starting the journey home an hour or two before dusk when he heard shouts up on a nearby hillside.

"He could see nothing from the valley but he was alarmed by the fear in the voice he heard. A man's voice, but pathetic somehow. He turned his horse from the path and spurred him as fast as he could go up the slope... "

Again Ludec hesitates and appears to be consulting the fire as to what happened next.

"Go on," prompts Gellick, his bread and cheese temporarily forgotten. "What did he find?"

"A monk was being set upon by two ruffians. They were bullying him for his crucifix and a few humble coins he had in his pocket for the market. My father leaped from his horse and drew his dagger hoping to scare the roughs off. Unfortunately they didn't run but turned on him instead. My father had a permanent scar down the left side of his face after that. A holy mark, the monk called it. Anyway, after a scuffle the pair fled empty handed and the monk wanted to give my father some sort of reward.

"Obviously he wouldn't think of it and declined the offer. But the monk – who was called Brother Jed – insisted on learning more about the man who had saved him. My father told him about me and Brother Jed immediately made plans to visit our farm to meet me.

"In fact he came back then and there with my father, the two of them on the same horse, and when he saw me he smiled and said he had a gift worth more than any amount of gold. He said he would teach me to read and write. And he did. He came once a week to see us, sometimes getting a lift on a pony or a cart, but often trekking for hours and hours just to fulfil his promise."

"Why didn't you go there, instead, with your father on his horse?" Gellick puts down his supper and quaffs a big, satisfying draft of Danish ale while he considers this point.

"The other monks wouldn't have allowed it, we were told," explains Ludec. "I don't know why. But from the age of six I had my own private tutor. My father naturally was delighted. Brother Jed taught me a lot of other things besides. And he would take nothing but our hospitality in exchange."

"A splendid reward for a virtuous man. Your father was very brave but you reaped a benefit that far outweighed his deed, methinks," says Etheld.

WHEN THE PREY JETJ THE TRAP

"I broke up a fight once," remembers Gellick thoughtfully. "All I got for it was a purpled eye."

* * * * *

Astrid spends fine April days strolling the pastures of her lonely manor-house with toddler Sky. She talks incessantly to her of her father, keeping him alive in her heart even though she is not yet old enough to understand everything she is saying. Sky knows only that she speaks of her daddy in a soft, hushed voice that shouts of love. It is Astrid's way of keeping him there, by their side.

Even with Sky, two servants and Claude, and her father and Beatrice not far away, Astrid has never felt lonelier. It is a different solitude from last year when Ludec was at least in the same country. Now his life was not only daily in mortal danger, but if he should fall in battle he would lay cold and loveless in a foreign land. It may be weeks before she hears of it.

Nonetheless there is hope in her heart, warmed by the spring sunshine that each sunrise grows stronger. She has heard that the Danish campaign has been successful and that the army will be returning soon to home shores. She smiles as she walks across the daisy mottled meadow-grass to where Claude stands in the doorway: where she had last espied him ever-watchful the day the messenger came, as aware of imminent danger as she. Her heart held a warm spot for him; he was indeed 'family'.

"I have a gift for you," he calls waving as she approaches, and she can see something white and black in his hands. He is beaming from ear to ear.

"I am surprised to see you," she jibes gently. "You spend so much time with Beatrice and my father on the farm."

She puts Sky down on the grass and watches her totter precariously towards Claude. "What have you got there?"

"Chess pieces." His smile is wide with pride. "I carved them myself from bone. Beatrice dyed the black."

"Let me see." Astrid is excited. Ludec taught her the rudimentary rules of the game but they never had a set of their own. They had played only once at the ale-house while they were courting. She weighs the delicately carved king and rook in her hand, feeling the balance and fingering the intricate contours. She smiles her delight. "Thank you, Claude. I never realised you were such an artist."

"And here... " he hands her a splendid white knight as tall as a man's middle finger, "is Sir Ludec."

She can't hold back her thrilled amazement as she recognises at once a spotted kerchief around the knight's neck. It is a tiny replica of one she herself gave him and which he often wears to show he is thinking of her.

"It's... it's wonderful. Thank you. Can we play?"

"Of course, but you had better ask Esther if she will watch the baby."

"Oh I think she can take an early nap. She's been chasing butterflies all morning."

Later as they sit just outside the door at a table playing on a makeshift board, a messenger once again arrives from Winchester.

Astrid looks up expectantly, keeping her heart light and her black fears at bay. "Good news? Is the army sailing home?"

The messenger throws the corner of his cloak back over his shoulder. "My Lady," he begins, respectfully lowering his eyes. "His eminence the King has made a new plan. The army is sailing north from Esbjerg this very week. They continue onward to conquer Sweden and Norway."

Astrid has been holding the white knight in her hand, in the middle of a move, and now her grip involuntarily releases it, and it tumbles to the floor where the finely carved head splinters at its neck.

In a shocked trance she stares down without comprehension at the spotted kerchief now freed from the restraints of its noble, helmed skull.

* * * * *

The King's new plan is total conquest of the Scandinavias, and onwards and upwards they sail, finally landing at the tip of Sweden. He believes this Haroldian Conquest is unstoppable, his army suffering hardly a scratch in nine months. In fact their numbers have been swollen by eager Viking conscripts.

Their armada is now joined by a small flotilla of the fearsome longboats, whose main advantage is that their shallower draft allows them access to bays and coves inaccessible to the bigger ships. This makes them a valuable asset for a surprise attack.

This is precisely how they launch their first attack on Sweden, with a feint soirée at night with the longboats, while 600 larger ships sail on until dawn to put in at Vaasen, a sizeable town on the coast. By the time the main fleet emerges like a sea spirit out of the morning mist, most of the defenders have been alerted in the middle of the night and gone to meet the Viking onslaught. Va'ard – for he is in command – has been instructed to withdraw back to his ships as soon as it is clear the bait has been taken.

"It worked – hardly anybody here," yells Gellick as the men put out the row-boats to head for shore. "They've headed west in force to meet Va'ard's Vikings."

Only a handful of the ships can pull into the harbour but they meet little resistance. Women, children and old men cower behind rag curtains in rough timber shacks and watch them approach. When they get too near, hands reach out to hastily close wooden shutters.

The town is taken without bloodshed.

"This trick will only work once," remarks Ludec as they take control of the township and organise it as a base.

"But won't their menfolk have a shock when they return?" Gellick is clearly impressed by his King's tactics.

Later that morning a small force of around 150 warriors limps back from their long fruitless walk westward to find their town in enemy hands. They too surrender without a fight and later that evening Va'ard's longboats arrive triumphant at the harbour entrance, a long winding fjord. Vaasen is thus secured and Harold puts his elaborate campaign in action. Within a week, his sprawling army meets the main Swedish force at a bleak, sparse pine forest a day's march away in the centre of the country.

"They call this a forest. Looks more like a pine needle swamp littered with one or two trees," observes Gellick as the three men line up together on their horses on the flank of the main battle line.

"Look at their pitiful numbers. They are less well armed than the poorest of our farm-boys." Etheld shoots an apologetic look across at Ludec for this sleight, but if any offence was taken none was shown. "I don't think the King will need our help this day."

"It will be over in an hour," Gellick continues. "They can't even hide in the trees. There's not one as thick as a slip of a wench."

At his command, the King's infantry advances on the pathetic Swedish line. His men are not only experienced, battle-hardened troops, but they have by now acquired the self-belief that wins wars as well as battles. There is much shouting and spear thrusting and swordplay but, as Gellick predicted, the Swedish line collapses almost at once. Their remnants pull back through the dour landscape towards a lake which will cut off further retreat.

"Harold can't use his bowmen for the trees," Etheld twists in his saddle to look back at the wasted rows of archers. Ludec is reminded of Arminius.

"And our horses can't climb them either," he says under his breath and his two friends look at him, mystified.

Inexplicably, Harold halts his advancing infantrymen and signals for the riders – split into two flanks either side of the battlefield – to bear down on the retreating Swedes.

Reluctantly, Etheld gives the order and 500 riders from each flank pour over the pine needle terrain, two galloping pincers which combine in the centre in front of their own cheering troops and then wheel to ride down the retreating Swedes. It is a bloody slaughter.

Ludec finds himself hacking blindly from left to right and back again for no better reason than he is expected to do it. He tries to shut his ears to the screams of those he and his friends are decapitating, dismembering and disembowelling. He just wants it over and this is the quickest way. He realises he is hardly ever in any kind of danger at all. At worse he faces a raised spear or sword, easily swept away with his own swirling, demonic blade.

WHEN THE PREY SETS THE TRAP

"For Albion," he screams but he knows his heart is empty. This is not for Albion, far less for Astrid and his child. This is for his King and his mad dreams of conquest.

"Albion forever," he hears from the mouth of Etheld at his side as he too cuts and parries and slices and hacks. And deep inside he knows he feels it too: the vacuous self-propaganda that is the knight's only way. This is not a fight for honour, or truth, or justice. This is no better than the bloodlust of the Vikings or the Normans. The only cause they serve is their King's and Ludec knows it is not enough.

Suddenly there is a sickening silence and Ludec stops his flailing arm because there is nothing left to cripple, maim or destroy. Bodies lay everywhere on the massive carpet of pine needles, bloodied, mutilated bodies of men and boys all the way down to the lake. Even there, Albion horsemen, their mounts up to their fetlocks in the wet, sit stock still in the saddle as they stare at the water streaked blood red near the shore. In their eyes, after the heat and insanity of battle, is only dazed surprise.

Then out of the silence comes a crescendo of cheers which Ludec realises comes from the stationary line of Albion infantrymen, still standing where they were ordered to halt.

"We have done God's work today," it is the King's strong voice, and Ludec looks up at him impassively as he canters across towards his now becalmed cavalry lines. "Sweden is ours."

Ludec wonders how this could ever be God's work and knows instinctively that William comforted himself with the self same lies when he embarked on his abortive invasion of Old Englande. God's work, Ludec thinks, but it is the devil who is laughing. He can hear him, between the thin trees; a rising crescendo of mirth that he realises at length comes from his own lines.

* * * * *

Two months later, Sweden and Denmark already flying the King's heraldic pennants, the Haroldian Conquest faces a tougher adversary. Norway is not only massive and mountainous, but the people less easily cowed. Vikings at heart, they have never before had to fear the blade of an invader.

Harold's vastly superior manpower has won the day in two small battles near the coast but now on June 15 1068, Albion is put to the test against a force of around 9,000 fierce, well-armed warriors.

"Have no care, lads," yells the King with his hallmark strong vocal chords as the two armies face each other on a warm, pleasant mountainside.

"We are invincible. YOU are invincible!" He rides up and down the lines, sword raised high in the air, as the cheers of his men ring in his ears. They love him, Ludec knows, and now they will follow him anywhere. They have tasted the spoils of war, the women, the looted wealth, and now they are hungry for more. Like a drug, it gets easier to spill blood the more you do it.

"I don't like this," murmurs Etheld for Ludec's ears only. "The Norwegians have the higher slope and we are left to struggle uphill. Our horses may be easily turned."

"I agree," considers Ludec. "My steed doesn't like climbing. He will arrive too exhausted to do anything but drop me in their laps."

It is early morning and even up here on the slopes the sun is already warm. Mid-summer flowers bedeck the meadowlands around them. A flock of sheep has wandered, oblivious, onto the coming battlefield. Ludec has a vision of bleating sheep and goats with their fleeces stained red. It is a ghastly, evil picture and he shakes his head to rid himself of it.

"Are you well?" asks Etheld, putting out an arm to steady his friend.

"Perhaps I should tell the King I'd rather like to give this one a miss," he smiles back. But his smile is thin and serious.

Ludec studies the Norwegian lines and can see no archers, just row upon row of sturdily built *Berserkers*, interspersed with stabbing spears, swords and axes.

"They are a bloody-looking lot," he adds and as he says this the swordsmen at the rear of the Norwegian lines start beating their round wooden shields with their blades, setting up a haunting and intimidating rhythm. Then, as one man, their front line begins to march slowly down the hill.

Harold has not been expecting this, Ludec realises. He has been used to more subservient prey of late.

Ludec and Etheld are centre of their lines, just behind the infantrymen whose brief is to stand aside if the order is given to allow the cavalry to charge through. Gellick, strangely, is nowhere to be seen and Ludec assumes he is with one of the other groups of riders further up or down the ranks.

"Archers!" goes up the cry and again Ludec hears the now familiar sounds of battle; the audible fussing and fidgeting as arrows are notched and strings pulled tight.

"Loose!" and the air thrums with the hideous purr of feathered flights, which can be heard even over the Norwegian drumming. It is Satan's symphony of death, a sound now as familiar to Ludec as the sound of birdsong in the morning.

So, too is the noise that follows; the drumming stops suddenly as shields are raised above heads, a tortoiseshell of protection for those quick enough. Then the clatter or ping of arrows that have missed their mark and have bounced harmlessly from metal rims or wooden shields. It's only the ones that don't miss that are silent – the only sound being the scream from its victim, already dying from a punctured chest.

Ludec tries to block out these terrible torments, which, although not common, are all the more spine-chilling for that. They are the unlucky few who forgot to duck and their cries pierce the strange, other-worldy silence as keenly as the arrows have pierced puny skin and bone. Ludec is sick of killing. More, he is sick of living to kill.

Through the morning the battle rages on as many have before, an advance, a retreat, a stalemate. Ludec thinks of the times he has tried to teach Astrid the basic moves of chess and marvels that women don't really have the stomach for it. They can learn the moves and win the battle, but they can rarely win the war.

He wonders if this anomaly betrays a deeper, unpalatable truth about the difference between the sexes. Women can enjoy the game, but generally lack the hardened resolve to consolidate a kill. Men

LUDEC

play to discover their opponent's weak points which they then use to thrust the dagger home.

By late afternoon, Ludec and Etheld find themselves literally bored in the saddle. They have not been called to charge as they might have expected, and there has been little to bother them, apart from occasional swarms of spears thrown clumsily from above. These are surprisingly easy to dodge, despite turning the blue sky dark with wooden shafts and glinting spear-points.

Then, the order comes, so suddenly that is a shock.

"Cavalry!" the yell goes up and down the line and Ludec wonders absurdly whether the men actually miss Orfur's elephantine trumpeting.

As if by magic the lines of infantry before them part to allow them to break through, and 1,000 horses begin to churn the battlefield with their hooves. Ludec finds himself yelling as he advances, spurring his steed to greater and greater speed with difficulty up the meadowland slope. He finds his way impaired by the wandering sheep, unfazed by the sounds of battle and intent only on chewing the short, succulent grass under their snouts.

"Mush! Mush" he implores, yet takes great care not to harm them with his sword or his horse's hooves. In the midst of battle, this strikes him as the ultimate irony. He can slice off a man's head yet balks at scratching the ugliest of goats.

His horse almost stumbles but regains its footing and they plough on back up the hillside to try to meet the enemy at full gallop. To his surprise the front ranks of Norwegian spearmen collapse almost immediately, falling away to the left and right under the onslaught of horse.

He can sense rather than hear the Albion infantrymen behind him being urged forward to take advantage of the gaps and soon he will have to watch whose neck he is severing. He wheels this way and that, his sword dealing death with a hunger that shocks him. Then even above the near-deafening din of battle comes the command for the cavalry to retreat. He immediately pulls back through his own advancing infantry who pour either side of him cheering and whooping as if battle was already won. He well knows it is just a soldier's way of spurring himself on and without it, he might just have time enough to think and decide to sit down right where he is in the grass and go no further.

Clear of the line, he wheels his horse around again for a better view of what's going on. The Albion infantry is indeed flowing like water through the collapsed Norwegian front lines, but there's something not quite right. The enemy spears, who so easily succumbed to the cavalry charge, are regrouping and closing the gaps behind the Albion front line. It is a feint, a trick, worthy of Harold's sneakiest. But Ludec's own men have not yet spotted it – they continue to chant and scream their way up the hill, unaware they are being locked in from their rear.

Worse, the King himself, enthused, has spurred his mighty warhorse forward and is joining his front lines which are becoming increasingly ensnared by the Norwegian cunning. He cannot see it is a trap, Ludec realises, and kicks his spurs deep into his steed's flanks.

"No sire," he screams at the top of his voice as he plunges through the closing lines of Norwegian spears. "It is a snare!"

He reaches the King's side and flails his blade wildly to protect him from the closing Norwegian ranks. Somehow Ludec notices the surprised look on his King's face; closely followed by a shocked realisation of what is really happening. Ludec is aware too that Etheld has also rushed to his side and they fight together like demons giving the King time and space to pull back to the Albion lines before the trap is fully set.

The King reaches the safety of his front lines, but is horrified to see that Etheld and his beloved Ludec are still ensnared.

"Cavalry!" The King yells desperately and again the horsemen plough back over the grassland, now churned to mud and blood, to destroy the Norwegian bear-trap.

He is just in time – the Norwegians once again fall screaming under the cavalry charge, and this time they are not pretending. But Etheld and Ludec are both unhorsed and out of sight of their King.

As the Albion cavalry drive the Norwegians further back up the hill, the scene is cleared and the King's heart breaks to see Ludec cradled in Etheld's arms on the ground, blood oozing from his upper body and groin. One leg is almost unrecognisable as a limb, hewn to ribbons by a score of lethal spear-points.

The King leaps from his horse and rushes to Ludec's side.

"Thank God you spotted the trap in time," he pants. "You saved my life – again. But my dearest Sir Ludec, you are badly hurt."

Ludec knows he will not live long. He is losing blood rapidly and something vital is punctured in his chest. A trickle of blood oozes from the corners of his mouth.

"Chase not the fox... lest you find... the wolf," he breathes and the King smiles sadly at the truth of his last words.

"You saw it clear, yet you gave your life to come to me," he whispers back, tears welling in his eyes. "Never has a king been so proud of a knight. Arthur could never have loved Lancelot so dear."

But Ludec is gone, his eyes closed peacefully against the battlefield carnage all around him. Etheld too is silenced by tears as he cradles Ludec's head in his arms.

"My knight. My friend," explodes the King and bows his head low over Ludec's body, tears falling like rain to mix with the blood on his chest.

Further up the hill, the Albion forces have finally routed the Norwegians. But the King's broken heart has surrendered unconditionally to deepest sorrow. He kneels in the blood and grass, an utterly vanquished victor.

CHAPTER NINE
A NATION MOURNS, JULY 1068

Harold concedes at last to return to Albion, if only so that the body of Sir Ludec can be laid to rest at home.

He has been crowned King of Denmark, Sweden and Norway all in one year, his wild dreams of conquest fully realised, yet it is a different man who sails up the Thames to London where Ludec is to be buried with honours at Westminster Abbey. When the abbey and castle at Winchester are finished, the remains of his friend and saviour will be moved there, to lie at the very heart of the Albion empire he did so much to forge.

Astrid and her daughter Sky, not yet two years old, are permitted to see the body and their tears mingle gently on his pallid cheeks. Astrid seeks what little comfort she can to ease their broken hearts. Ludec has loved and become a national hero in protecting that love – what greater epitaph can a man wish for?

"He was a farmer first and a hero second," she tells her bewildered daughter as they gaze into the serene face in the open coffin. Astrid is saddened to note that the spotted scarf she gave him is missing.

"But beyond all else he was my husband and your father."

The nation ostentatiously mourns. Black bunting is draped from every building up and down the land. A statue of his likeness, by one of the finest sculptors in Europe, is commissioned for Winchester cathedral where it will flank Harold's own. An imagined likeness of Arthur – the Once and Future King, will stand on the King's right side, Ludec on his left.

"Would it please the King if Ludec's likeness is remembered with his 'kerchief? It was a love token from me and he promised to wear it always." Astrid now finds her relationship with the King strained and difficult, she blaming Ludec's death on his lust for power and conquest. But she is touched to have been consulted over plans to erect a statue in Ludec's honour.

"Yes, of course. I recall it well. He wore it always." The King has a different persona from just a year earlier. His bloodlust and the consequent death of Albion's most beloved hero has aged him prematurely and he stands before her now a faintly lugubrious old man, although still only in his forties.

"My Lady Astrid... " begins the King awkwardly, but she curtsies pre-emptively and turns to leave without a word, which would be unforgiveable from anyone else. But the King, hurt though he is, understands both her grief and her blame.

"My court and my Kingdom are yours," he continues to her back as Astrid walks away. "You shall want for nothing. Would you not care to travel back to Winchester with the Royal Entourage?"

Astrid ignores the deep bows of the lackeys as she leaves the cold, stone walls of Westminster Abbey and returns to an ante-room where Claude and Sky are waiting.

Silently they step out into the mid-summer sunshine and climb into a rough wooden cart pulled by two impatient horses. Claude takes the reins and they begin the long trek back to Winchester in quiet contemplation of devastating loss.

Back inside the abbey, Sir Etheld does his best to comfort his King after Astrid's snub.

"She means not to be unkind or rude," he says. "Her manners lie hidden and forgotten under layers of grief."

The King waves a dismissive hand. "There is nothing to forgive save what I have done. Sir Ludec stemmed my impetuosity and in so doing probably single-handedly saved Albion from the brutalities of an invader.

"Who knows what bleak depths our nation could have plumbed under the tyranny of a Norman conqueror? It doesn't even bear thinking about. I think I can forgive his widow a minor lapse of etiquette. But whether she can ever forgive me, now that is another question."

Astrid and Sky continue to live an unimaginably privileged lifestyle at their manor house, the King proving true to his word and never forgetting his trusted lieutenant.

Harold himself grows mellow and insular as he grows older, content to let his past glories testify to his greatness. No longer in the shadow of his forbear King Alfred, the monarch previously attributed with the Arthurian qualities of legend and lore. Harold now believes he IS the Once and Future King reborn.

When Winchester cathedral and castle are finally completed, the knights take their places at the Round Table in the Great Hall, Sir Etheld at the head before the fire and opposite him a special chair always to be kept vacant. Engraved in gold at its back is the name of its owner, Sir Ludec.

"He will watch over us forever," says the King quietly. "He will advise wisely and so guide our spirit that we shall always do right for Albion and her peoples."

The King is proud of his nation's gratitude to him for saving them from conquest and for the glory of annexing the Scandinavias under the Greater Albion banner.

Yet he knows it was not without cost, and every time he glances at the empty chair at the Round Table he feels it keenly.

"Ludec was proud to die at your side and by his death to save you," persists Sir Etheld, for he sees that the King's grief is inexorably eating away at his fleeting sense of glory.

In March 1073 Ludec's statue is finally placed on the concourse of Winchester Cathedral as promised, his spotted kerchief about his neck for all to see. With Arthur, he stands alongside the King he served so well. But when Astrid and Sky gaze proud and lovingly at the statue, they see not the fluttering, brash, imperial banners but Astrid's simple token of love, the flag under which he truly fought.

Albion continues to flourish and prosper while the Norman epoch dies a lingering and merciless death by the sword as it had sought to perpetuate itself.

LUDEC

"The Norman dynasty is imploding, falling victim to other French noblemen who covet its lands," emissaries tell Harold at his court in Winchester. They see before them a strangely broken man, despite all his achievements, and they hope the news will cheer him.

"They continued to flourish briefly but spectacularly in Italy and even in the east, but now they are a dying light whereas Albion burns bright as a beacon. Her future is assured, thanks to you, good King."

"I... and others," replies Harold but the assembled emissaries can hardly hear his mumbling. It is not for their ears, it is for Ludec's.

Within a few decades, the only Norman enclave left intact in the world is ironically on the Isle of Wit, little more than a stone's throw from the Albion capital of Winchester. But Harold needs have no fear: these Normans insinuate themselves into peaceful, community life becoming more Albion than Albion.

Albion is now an omnipotent force in the developing world, confident and proud of its abilities, commanding respect and admiration from traders everywhere, not just from Europe but from the great, wide continents beyond. She is rich in minerals, learning and commerce, richer still in spirit.

Harold dies contented yet haunted in 1085 and two generations of Albion Kings after him, Erlik and his son Obin, continue to ensure Denmark, Norway and Sweden stay in the fold by embarking on a further invasion of Finland.

They are costly wars but Albion's wealth is now beyond measure in Europe and the annexing of Finland means that Scandinavia is boxed in from all sides. From that century forward, they never think of themselves as anything other than citizens of Greater Albion.

Astrid outlives the King by 10 years and dies peacefully at her Winchester country home, content to have remained a warrior hero's widow.

Claude has married Beatrice, despite their age difference, and remains on the farm after the death of Astrid's father Egbert.

Resigned yet fulfilled, Astrid breathes her last deathbed words to Sky, who has grown into a beautiful young woman.

"Find a man like your father; unconquerable not because of any sword or mace, but because of the power of his love. He loved his nation, but he loved us more."

A NATION MOURNS, JULY 1068

Sky eventually marries a Scottish nobleman she meets at court and lives a long and happy life on the western isles. Each of her two children, whom she names Ludec and Astrid, are blessed with their mother's striking blue eyes. She tells them stories of a handsome hero called Sir Ludec and of a mysterious Dark Matter ingot that nobody can see, but which can itself see all.

It is perhaps waiting, like a child playing hide and seek, to be recognised and understood.

CHAPTER TEN

THE DARK MATTER BOMB

"... From Its Heart All Things Are Made"

June 1936. The Albion Museum, Winchester. Lily presses her nose close to the glass and turns her head this way and that, puckering up her lips to breathe a misty cloud of condensation in which she traces two words with her finger: "Skool Unkool."

"Press the button, Lily," encourages her father, a casually dressed man in a dark blue suit, jacket unbuttoned and tie permanently loosened around his neck.

Lily takes a step back from the huge, reinforced display case to investigate the button. Locating it almost at once, she presses eagerly with the thumbs of both hands.

"Daddy, it's disappeared!" she exclaims excitedly as the lighting in the cubicle alters leaving the engraved silver casket suddenly empty, where before there was a glossy, black ingot. "Is it magic?"

Ludec Strong's striking blue eyes sparkle enthusiastically as he thrills at the workings of his daughter's 10-year-old mind. As a journalist he is necessarily interested in people, but since he and Alicia had Lily, he is constantly bemused by this entirely new species presented to him.

"No, not magic exactly. But for centuries everyone believed it was."

"Like electricity?"

"Exactly."

"And the Ford Hoverer?"

"Yes."

THE DARK MATTER BOMB

But Lily is already bored and hungry for something different. She skips over to another showcase and peers inside at three bone chess pieces. The white knight has lost his head. She peers at the label and struggles with the unfamiliar lettering.

"What's 'Circa 11th Century'? Is it from a circus?"

Ludec wanders over more slowly and peers inside. He has seen it all before.

"It means 'around the time of'." He stoops to read the small print. "This was found on the site of a former manor house near here. A farmer's plough dug it up. That's likely to be what damaged it. The rest has never been found."

Ludec thinks his daughter, who is shielding the glare with her two hands against the glass and her forehead, is about to butterfly to the next display case.

Instead she intones: "Daddy!" and Ludec knows to stand by for more startling revelations from an inspired, one decade-old mind. He isn't disappointed.

"The knight has got a patterned scarf like the statue of you outside Winchester Cathedral."

"That isn't me, sweet pea. We just have the same name. THAT Ludec lived 1,000 years ago." Nevertherless he moves in closer to investigate.

"Hmmm," he concedes. "Never noticed that before."

They wander around happily for the rest of the afternoon while Alicia is at her dance class. They will all meet later and take tea on the Winchester Wheel with its staggering views over the capital.

The fabulous 700-feet high wheel is Albion's joyous celebration of DM technology. Fifty-two brightly lit glass coaches gently circle without benefit of spoke or hub, a sight to take the breath away. The conjured coaches – one for every week of the year – revolve as if by magic bathed in colour according to the seasons, from dazzling white for winter, through to pale green, then deep green and finally yellow ochre bleeding into bright orange for highest summer. They gradually fade to gold and burnt umber for deepening autumn.

DM technology has freed the world from the restrictive yoke of gravity, allowing architecture to literally take wing. Apartment blocks, offices and houses now breathe a surreal existence of their own, hanging miraculously and independently in thin air with no apparent link to terra firma. Traditionalist builders still cling to the earth as if for comfort, but avant garde architects, like children playing, refuse to keep excited feet on the ground. Modern cities – of which proud Winchester generally is not – sprouted almost overnight into a floating fiesta of dizzying abstraction.

And the benefits are not all earthbound; Albion's scientists are confident they will put a man on the moon by 1940. And then – who knows? The entire universe will be just a hop, skip and a jump away.

It is already theoretically possible to 'fly' instantly to the moon by DM transporter, but reception and despatch stations are required at either end. United world space programmes are accelerating plans to first cover the quarter of a million miles by 'old fashioned' jet propulsion. DM transportation currently exists on earth but is available only to the ridiculously super-rich.

But today Ludec is drawn as always to the beautifully bound and illustrated book by the 11th century monk Brother Jed. What little the world knows about Sir Ludec can be found in its pages. He lived such a short life, dying at the age of 24. Brother Jed was a Benedictine monk who apparently taught him to read and write and dedicates an entire chapter to young Ludec's life on a Sussex farm. It is a fascinating insight for Ludec who secretly suspects they may have been related, but has never found any genealogical evidence. It was just a 'feeling', strange but undeniably substantial.

Lily is not much interested in the book. It reminds her too much of school which, today, a Saturday, she is glad to be freed from. She flips here and there, just like her flibbertigibbet synapses, excited and absorbed for a mere split second, before becoming disinterested and yielding to a compunction to move on to the next exciting Wonder of the World. That's the most beautiful thing about her 10-year-old brain, Ludec knows: everything is a Wonder of the World, however briefly. He thinks of the mayfly and of hungrily cramming everything in as if there is no tomorrow which, if you are a mayfly, there isn't. Maybe not for Lily, either. Or for anyone else. His thoughts turn dark and he hastens to change the mood as completely as possible.

"Seen enough? Let's go and meet mummy."

Later that same evening Ludec is talking softly to Lily as she snuggles down in her bed for the night.

"Can I read?"

"Of course, but don't forget to turn off the light."

"I won't. But Daddy... " mention of the light had reminded her of something.

"Yes?"

"Why did the inglynut disappear when they switched the light? It had to be a clever trick, didn't it?"

Ludec pulls her cartoon puppy duvet up around her neck as she settles down. He knows this is going to take some time. He never shirks when her appetite for knowledge needs feeding. She is bright and a bright mind needs challenge.

"For centuries they thought it was a trick," he says. "It is supposed to have come from Merlin's cave, and when men looked at it they mostly couldn't see it... "

"Merlin is in the King Arthur stories, isn't he?"

"Yes. Which may or may not be nothing but legend. But the Dark Matter ingot – I-N-G-O-T – *(he spells it out for her)* shows that the ancients indeed knew more than we did for centuries. It shows up as a cursory mention, almost a rumour, in the writings of Brother Jed, but really nothing was known about it until 1910."

"That's when the Henry T Ford motor car was made! "

"Yes and within 20 years the first Ford Hoverer took to the skies – and all because of Merlin's Dark Matter ingot."

"All because of the inglynut? But what is it?"

"The *ingot*, yes. Let me tell you all about it. It is a fascinating story."

Just then Alicia peers around the door. "Ludy, she ought to be getting to sleep. She's had a busy day."

Ludec turns to her from his position perched on the side of Lily's bed. "I'm afraid I've got a two-page special on here. Lights off is delayed."

Alicia looks pretend-stern and taps her watch. "Well, consider it an eight-o-clock deadline. Thirty minutes."

Ludec and his daughter exchange a smile. She is eager to hear all about the inglynut. Her Daddy tells it all so much clearer than she hears it at school.

"The ingot disappeared from the face of the earth for centuries. Brother Jed tells us that it was at least rumoured to exist in Sir Ludec's time *(Lily loves to hear about Sir Ludec; she too fervently wants to believe he was an ancestor)* but it was the monarchy's best-kept secret.

"Anyway across the centuries there was never another hint of it until 1910."

"What happened then?"

"Shh, I'm just telling you. A team of archaeological divers was looking for King Elrik the Second's lost treasure in The Wash."

"Had it got dirty?"

Ludec smiles. He loves his daughter's brain. Sometimes he feels that it is she who is enlightened, not he.

"The Wash is an estuary off the coast of Norfolk. King Elrik the Second was supposed to have lost his Crown Jewels there in 1216. There were many attempts to find the lost treasure but they were hampered by fuzzy information. Then in 1910 a team from Cambridge University got lucky.

"They dug up a hoard of jewels, including the silver casket you saw today in the museum. The inscription read: 'Tho' this ingot cans't be weigh'd, from its heart all things are made.' But inside it was empty. Or so they thought. It was sent with other artefacts..."

"Are those facts painted by an artist?" Lily wants to know.

"... to the historical boffins at Cambridge University. There they noticed something very odd. Every now and again, something would become briefly visible inside the casket... "

"The inglynut!" shouts Lily excitedly.

"The ingot, yes. So it is sent in turn to the university's scientific laboratories and within two years they made a breakthrough with a new modern invention – laser technology."

"That's light, isn't it? Special light?"

"Simply put, yes," says Ludec. "Scientists discovered a way to make the ingot clearly visible so they could study it, as you saw for yourself today."

"Ludy!" Alicia's worried voice carries up from the landing. "Don't keep her up too long."

"I need to hear this," Lily shouts down to her mother, and Alicia reluctantly leaves them alone. Turning back to her father she asks again: "But what IS it?"

"Scientists have known for a long time that the properties we understand about the world, the *building blocks* of existence, amount to very little. If you are given a whole barrel of strawberries, then just one strawberry would represent all we know about the universe we live in."

He pauses for Lily's silently mouthed "wow!". "So if it's so little how come my teachers are so long-winded about it?" she interrupts but her father is in full flow.

"By far the majority of everything around us – most of it - is made up of something called Dark Matter. For the first time scientists were able to study it and world technology took a huge leap forward overnight."

"Is that how we got the Hoverer?"

"Yes, and much more besides. Not all of it good."

"What are the bad things?"

"We don't want to talk about that now. Just remember that the discovery led to huge changes in the way we live – medicine and surgery, transport, space technology, everything. "

"All because of Merlin's... " began Lily, looking at last a touch sleepy eyed.

"Ingot. I-N-G-O-T. Now it's time for dreams, my little darling." He leans over to kiss her goodnight but she is already asleep, a contented smile on her face.

Later, downstairs, Alicia asks what they had been talking about that had held Lily so spellbound.

"She wanted to know all about Dark Matter."

"You didn't lecture her on the bomb?" Alicia knows he didn't, she's just making conversation. She knows about the darkness in

Ludec's past and has forgiven him. He paid a high price in a prison cell. She just finds herself double checking sometimes.

"Of course not. But she's eager to learn about everything. It's amazing. You know what? She even spotted something I had never noticed at the museum today."

Alicia looks at him, interested.

"You know those white chess pieces they dug up from a field somewhere? Lily noticed that the knight had a patterned handkerchief or scarf around his neck just like the statue at the cathedral."

"Which statue?"

"Sir Ludec. The knight who saved Albion from a Norman conquest in 1067."

"Meaning what, exactly?" Alicia is mystified.

"Well, it may mean nothing. Perhaps such kerchiefs were all the rage at the time. But it may mean... "

"... that the chess piece was supposed to be him," Alicia finishes for him, suddenly excited herself. "That's amazing. Do you think anyone else has ever thought about it?"

"Maybe I'll write a piece," Ludec muses and Alicia smiles to herself. She knows Ludec is fixated with the idea he may actually be distantly related to the knight though the name is not uncommon these days for obvious reasons.

"You know you are a bit like Sir Ludec in many ways," she goes on, playfully pandering to his obsession. "He saved Albion by warning the King not to rush too early into a battle with the Normans and you write articles warning Albion not to rush into war with the Rhinelanders and that evil fascist Hildebrand. Maybe you were both chasing your own Holy Grail, in not so very different ways?"

Ludec ponders this for a moment. Alicia is right. There is a small connection which nonetheless should not be ignored.

"So you'd better tell me more about what you told Lily this evening," Alicia teases. "I don't want to be branded a dunce at the tea table tomorrow."

"I just explained more about Merlin's ingot. She couldn't be bothered with it much when we were at the museum – I think she was more interested in getting to the Wheel with you. But tonight she had obviously been mulling it over."

Alicia looks concerned. "Well, I don't really know much about the Dark Matter bomb either. Only that it's here now – threatening us all. Oh God, Ludy, is it as bad as you make it sound? There hasn't been a major war for literally centuries. So why is the DM bomb so dangerous? It is supposed to help keep the peace, isn't it?"

"The DM bomb has only just been developed in the last couple of years, eclipsing early attempts in Albion and the USNA to split the atom. When the scientists started to dabble with anti-matter they opened a whole Pandora's Box of destruction. The A-bomb and the H-bomb would not have been developed for decades yet, perhaps never, if the world hadn't found how to dabble with Dark Matter.

"Now nuclear bombs, dependent on nuclear fission, are commonplace but technically quite vulgar compared to the DM bomb. Albion researchers at Cambridge University split the atom at just about the same time as Lars Neisson cracked DM at Oxford. His bomb doesn't explode – it evaporates everything. Cleanly, efficiently and totally."

Alicia is determined to show she can at least keep up. "Molecules just revert back to whichever anti-matter properties they'd least like to be, I believe you wrote somewhere. A sort of nothingness. Not that I understood that, either."

"It's decidedly more complicated than nuclear fission," agrees Ludec. "The discovery of the DM ingot spurred on research already being carried out on positrons and neutrons which had only just been discovered. It is quantum physics with a capital question mark.

"Only last year a Rhinelander physicist Erwin Schrodinger carried out an outrageous experiment called Schrodinger's cat in which he tried to demonstrate that in quantum mechanics a cat could be deemed dead and alive at the same time. I didn't understand it entirely myself."

Alicia looks troubled. "Wasn't that more of a case of semantics? It seemed that way to me."

"Possibly," concedes Ludec. "The concept is tough to follow. But there are other experiments that truly show what a mind-blowing riddle it all is. And Dark Matter is quite the biggest part of that riddle.

It's not all new. A physicist called Thomas Young was conducting baffling experiments suggesting mysterious quantum properties of light as early as 1803. Scientists knew such unanswered questions were out there, but it wasn't until they were able to study the Dark Matter ingot that the light finally shone."

"Or didn't shine," adds Alicia and Ludec smiles wryly.

"Great men have called it dabbling with the workings of God and perhaps he alone knows where it will all end.

"Now we not only have atom bombs and hydrogen bombs but dark matter bombs just in case we forget to light a fuse somewhere. It's madness. And all it takes to set it all off is someone like this Rhinelander fascist Hildebrand who is threatening to take over huge tracts of Europe."

"Your column really helps, Ludy, I'm convinced of it. People may not always like it, but it makes them think. They need shaking up. The more they shout insults like 'apologist' and accuse you of cowtying, the more you know you are getting through. It takes genuine bravery for a pacifist to countenance peace when people perceive it as cowardice – Sir Ludec found that out."

"I wouldn't describe myself as a pacifist, exactly," counters Ludec. "But posturing, sabre-rattling days are long gone. The end-game is Armageddon. In just a couple of years the technology has spread across the world. Free Mongolia has it, the USNA have it, even the Terra-del-Basques have it."

"Not forgetting Hildebrand," reminds Alicia regretfully.

"Yes and now it looks as if she wants to kick-start the first world war with it. I know one thing," adds Ludec. "The first world war will also be the last world war."

Suddenly Ludec and Alicia both look up as a small voice calls from upstairs.

"Daddy! Mummy!"

"She's having nightmares about ingots," says Alicia accusingly as she gets up from the white leather sofa.

"Inglynuts," corrects Ludec.

CHAPTER ELEVEN
THE EVE OF THE GREAT WAR

September 14, 1936: The Eve of the Great War

As a newspaperman with the Albion Daily Trumpet, Ludec Strong reads his own morning paper with curiously detached dismay.

CHASE THE FOX, BUT BEWARE THE HUNGRY WOLF
By Ludec Strong, Chief Reporter
A thousand years of peace is about to explode into World War. And why? Because some tin-pot she-devil is getting too big for her cloven hooves, that's why. But before you run up the flag and shout Gung-Ho, remember this. If we rush into a World War now, it will be the last one we ever have. It will be the last anything we ever have. Enjoy your breakfast.

Ludec throws the paper in the pavement disposal unit and hails a free Hovercar. "The Nugget," he snaps moodily.

He can see the driver straining to get a better look at him in his mirror. Ludec shifts uncomfortably in his seat. He is in no mood for this.

"You're that Luddie Strong fellow, ain't yuh? Read your stuff every day."

Ludec remains silent and deadpan, staring out the window at the road gliding silently by beneath.

But the driver is thick skinned. "What I want to know is, what the hell else do we do if we don't stand up to her? Tell me that."

LUDEC

Ludec has no answer. He has no answers at all anymore.

"Sorry, friend. I just want to get to the bar and throw a stiff one down the back of my throat."

"Don't get me wrong, Mr Strong. I see your point. But I think you're getting yourself a bit of a reputation – the wrong sort of reputation, if you take my meaning... "

Luckily for Ludec, the cab is drawing up outside the Nugget and is hissing gently back down to the pavement.

He slips five albis into the driver's hand as he climbs out. Maybe that will be enough to win back his fan base.

The taxi-pilot was talking about Chancellor Hildebrand of Rhineland who has been posturing menacingly for months about enemies within tainting pure-blood Aryans. She rants noisily about Jews and gypsies, but in reality she means anyone who isn't a Rhinelander.

Ludec, with his bright, piercing blue eyes, is a popular figure in the newsroom, although when he withdraws deep within himself, thoughtful, he can appear a little sullen. He likes a drink, too, but most reporters do.

He often speculates but could never prove that he might actually be related to the Sir Ludec whose famous statue stands on the concourse at Winchester cathedral. That Ludec (1044 – 1068) is described on the plinth as "The Hero of Albion's Finest Hour" who famously advised Harold to wait rather than rush into battle against the would-be Norman conqueror William.

Amazing how history repeats itself, Ludec thinks now.

Little else was known about the shining white knight as he died very young in the Haroldian campaigns against the ancient nations once known as Norway and Sweden. He was killed in action aged only 24.

"What frightens me," says Ludec to his closest editorial chums around the bar in the Winchester Nugget, "apart from war itself, what other alternative is there? I feel just like that 11th century Sir Ludec, counselling the King against taking up the sword. But the root problem is; there's really no choice."

Ludec has had a beer or two it's true. But he is in a particularly despondent mood.

"Cheer up," beams Edwin, trying to catch the barman's attention for another round. "Might never happen."

"Wish that were the truth," mumbles Ludec, cuddling his big pint tankard before him. "How I wish that was the truth."

Edwin orders the drinks and slips three Albis across the slippery, beer-sodden counter. "Come on, Luddie. Our boys will sort her out before it comes to a big showdown. She'll see we mean business and won't be ranting for long once good old Albion takes a swing at her most unlovely chin."

"Luddie may be right," says Christian Kristerssen. "She's got the DM bomb too. What happens if she is mad enough to use it? We ALL go up in a puff of smoke." He catches the barman's eye and gestures with his head and raised eyebrows for a packet of crisps from the shelf behind him.

"Now that's the real bazooma," moans Ludec. "She probably IS mad enough to use it. Believe me she's got designs on all Europe. It'll all go up in a puff of smoke. A thousand years of peace – pfffttt! Just like that."

"Oh, come on, Luddie. Here's 50 albis to say it'll come to nothing. She wouldn't dare." Edwin is the first to slap his money on the counter. He's also the last.

An hour or two later Ludec slips rather ungracefully off his stool, leaving his fourth pint unfinished on the bar. "Going home," he says. "While I've still got one."

His chums raise their glasses to him as he stumbles somewhat towards the door. "Pfffttt!" says Christian as a kind of goodbye salute.

"Nobody is taking it seriously," a more sober Ludec later tells his wife Alicia at their out-of-town farmhouse. "They all think it's a huge joke, but it isn't."

Alicia knows better than to argue. Politics is his province, not hers. If he says it's a worrying situation then, as far as she is concerned, it is.

Alicia is pregnant with their second child and Ludec is secretly considering sending her and Lily off to her sister's in the Brecon Beacons. He's got to stay here, with his paper, but she might be safer there. Maybe. Or there's her cousin in the USNA, or is it the Confederates? He can't remember.

"What can we do?" she asks softly, her arm lovingly around his shoulders and gently massaging his neck.

"Pray," says Ludec simply. "Just pray."

Within weeks, Ludec is raking in the bets from his pals on the editorial floor. Rhineland has invaded Slavia, poor defenceless Slavia.

"Here's your 50 albis," says Edwin begrudgingly in the unusually hushed newsroom. "I never thought it would go this far."

"Keep it." Ludec looks sullen. His mind is racing and all he can think about is Lily and Alicia and their unborn child. This is no time for a war. "Buy yourself a ticket to the moon. It's the only place any of us might be safe."

In the background a wide-screen TV flickers ominously with scenes of tanks and heavy armaments pouring unchecked over Slavic border-posts.

Suddenly behind them a window smashes as a bottle is hurled through it. The Trumpet is on the third floor, so it had to be a pretty lucky shot.

Editorial staff move warily to the broken window and stare out onto the street below. Ludec joins them and is horrified to see a large, chanting crowd waving banners.

"BURN THE TRUMPET – DON'T BLOW IT!" screams one.

And another: "LOONY STRONG IS A SNIVELLING APPEASER!"

As the voices in the street grow even louder, a brick breaks another window and there is an alarmed cry from one or two of the girl secretaries. Reporters move in gallantly to clear up the slivers of glass.

"Luddie, would you mind?" it is Kris Austin, the editor, a worried half-smile on his face. Behind him in the glass-windowed editor's office stands Prentice the publisher, waiting. It is still early autumn and quite warm, but Prentice looks sternly incongruous in a heavy tweed overcoat, an unlit cigar in his mouth. Ludec can see he is a man on a mission.

Without a word he follows Kris into his office and the ugly sounds in the street are mercifully silenced by the closing of the door behind them.

"Sit down." Kris is trying to sound matter-of-fact but the words still come across as an order. Prentice remains where he is on his feet, hands deep in his pocket. He says nothing. Kris slumps into his green, leather-upholstered, captain's chair the other side of the desk.

"Luddie, it's inevitable." His expression is pained.

Ludec looks down at his lap. He has nothing to say. And neither has the publisher – Ludec knows he's going to let the editor say it for him.

"Mr Prentice is of the opinion that, well, The Trumpet has been... *wrong*... in allowing so many column inches for an anti-war stance..." he pauses and reaches for a cigarette, lighting it from a Merlin's Nugget desk lighter without offering the pack around. Absent mindedly he presses the mahogany plinth and the nugget lighter disappears.

"He... we..." Kris has something heavy to say and Ludec can feel the weight of it before his tongue can even spit out the words. He has a pretty fair idea of what's coming.

"What your editor is trying to tell you," says Prentice suddenly, taking his hands out of his pockets and leaning them instead on the desk to loom menacingly over them both, "is that The Trumpet will no longer tolerate your pacifist piffle. Whatever your motives, and I have known you a long time and have no doubt at all about your integrity, you are seen by our five million readers as a damned apologist.

"We overlooked your... *unfortunate*... past once because we believed in you, in your passion and your drive. But we can't keep tolerating your failings. I'm afraid you are proving to be too much trouble."

Ludec raises his eyes defiantly to meet the publisher's. Much more of this and he will find out just how much of a pacifist he really is. Prentice continues to prattle on but Ludec is aware only of the dancing muscle movements in his jaw, and how tempting a target for his fist those big, mincing jowls are.

"Listen to the voices in the street, Ludec." The publisher's tone has changed suddenly as if to feather-bed the hostility he has inadvertently created. "We can't be seen as a toadying Trumpet – we have to show the country that we will not put up with Hildebrand or any other threat to world peace, whatever the cost."

"Whatever the cost?" repeats Ludec lamely, but he feels just as lame as he sounds.

The editor coughs politely to interrupt for a moment. "We gave you a lot of license, Luddie, while there was a chance that it would all blow over. But now the chips are down. War is inevitable... today, tomorrow? Who knows? But it's no good wasting valuable editorial space on a lost cause."

"You want to stop campaigning for peace?" Ludec is responding to his editor but is staring Prentice straight in the eye.

"I'm afraid Mr Prentice would like you to step down. At least until after it is all over." Ludec looks shocked and Kris adds hurriedly: "This is not a sacking. You can come back. But we'd like you to lay low for the duration."

"*Come back*?" Ludec now sounds as stunned as he looks. "*Come back?* For Christ's sakes, Kris, there'll be no bloody Trumpet to *come back* to. There'll be no bloody *anything* to come back to."

He gets up and storms out of the office only vaguely aware of his editor's half-hearted attempts to stop him. He barges past alarmed colleagues, who have been watching the wordless events through the glass panes, and heads straight to the lift and out onto the street.

"Luddie!" is the last thing he hears as he leaves the carpeted, aspidistra comfort of the office that has been his second home for the past 10 years.

"Traitor!" is the first thing he hears as he steps out into the autumn sunshine. "It's Loony Ludec. Get him!"

The mob gathered beneath the Trumpet offices is seething with anger. A woman with a placard proclaiming "HILDEBRAND'S (S)TRUMPET" stumbles towards him and crashes the whole thing over his head. It breaks easily, but the thin plywood splinters into tiny pieces, covering him with nasty, prickling shards.

"Get him!" The cry goes up again, angrier this time, and Ludec breaks into a run. He sprints blindly towards the left where the crowd is thinnest and is gratefully aware of a Hovercar hissing down at his side. He climbs in breathless and it elevates immediately, humming away to safety.

"Where to, Mr Strong? The Nugget?"

Ludec recognises the voice immediately. It is marvellous what a five-albi tip will do.

* * * * *

September 17th, 1936, the entire human race holds its breath on the eve of what has already been dubbed The First World War, The Great War.

The Nazi Republic of Rhineland has poured its troops and tanks into Western Slavia, a country considered a cousin state of the Albion Republic Commonwealth and the world waits for Winchester's official reaction.

This is the Albion Broadcasting Corporation Home Service. It is 10 o'clock. Here is the news...

A voice, so grave it is almost moribund, intrudes into the momentary silence as millions huddle around radios in kitchens and sitting rooms, not just in Albion, but across the globe.

This is your President Edica. I am speaking to you now from the Presidential Palace in Winchester and I have just come from a meeting with your Government here at Camelot House.

As you are aware, 48 hours ago Chancellor Hildebrand of Rhineland ordered an unprovoked invasion of Western Slavia. Today storm-troopers have subjugated those peaceful peoples in contravention of every law known to man, moral and writ.

Last night this Government informed the Rhineland Chancellor that if those forces were not withdrawn by 8.00am today then there would follow serious, dire consequences.

I have to tell you that no such undertaking has been received so as of this morning a state of war now exists between us.

There is panic in the streets. Frightened children hug their parents, lovers clutch each other knowing this may be their last embrace. Old men shake their heads, resigned.

Christian and Edwin, from the paper, are sitting with Ludec and his family in their farmhouse sitting room. Light orchestral music now playing soothingly on the radio fails to lift the gloom.

"What the hell?" Christian looks from face to face as Edwin lets out a long, low whistle through his teeth. "How could it ever come to this?"

They all know that Ludec was almost alone in seeing this coming and a host of unspoken questions are directed at him.

"Rhineland has been stock-piling its military might for decades," says Ludec on cue. "But, frankly, nobody took much notice. All eyes have been on the gargantuan Mongolian empire. They have the most modern, hi-tech fighting machine on the planet."

Edwin pipes in: "An army said to exceed 20 million."

Ludec nods his agreement. "But they were never perceived as an imminent threat. Why covet the paddling pool when you own the beach? Now these radical Rhinelanders have turned European politics on its head. The Nazis are on the march and, believe me, Caesaria will be next to join up."

He turns to Alicia who is sitting across from him, her arm around Lily who is standing in front of her and listening to every word.

"Whatever happens it is going be one hell of a mess around here," he tells her. "I don't want to sound pessimistic, but I don't want to risk you being here if Rhineland invades."

"Invades? Here?" Alicia is incredulous.

"It's unlikely, but it could happen. So I want you to take Lily and go to your cousin in the USNA."

"Actually she lives in the CSA, Tennessee," she replies and, shivering, adds "and anyway I hate flying. I'd rather go to Katie in the Brecon Beacons."

"If there's an invasion nowhere in Albion will be safe," says Ludec sternly. "You'll have to take the DM flight."

"Oh, Luddie, you know we could never afford that. And anyway it spooks me out."

Dark Matter technology has also brought with it transportation involving anti-matter transference. Passengers – none but the rich and famous – board at a DM Port, the door is shut and, presto, they're there: instantaneously. You step in near Maidstone in Kent and step out again in Michigan a fraction of a second later.

"Great way of travelling light – especially in the wallet," jokes Christian. They each know one seat costs the equivalent of a journalist's yearly wage. It'll soon be cheaper to take a pleasure trip around the moon, the old-fashioned way using rocket propulsion.

Just as the Dark Matter bomb has rendered the atomic age obsolete, so too has DM energy revolutionised travel.

But from her body language it is clear Alicia has no intention of going anywhere.

"Ludec has been filling the paper with all this for months, and nobody would listen," she says, leaning over from her sofa and stretching out to take his hand. "Lily and I aren't leaving. We will stay here with Daddy as a family, won't we Lily? Even if it's all too late." Sadly, Lily hugs her mum and also reaches over to touch Ludec's arm to show her support.

"Maybe it's not quite all over," adds Ludec mysteriously. "Perhaps Merlin's Ingot may still have a surprise or two in store for us yet, if we're lucky."

* * * * *

For the next day or two there is saturation media coverage on Albion's military preparations for war. Caesaria looks increasingly likely to wade in on the side of the Fascists and prospects look bleak.

Militarily, Albion rules both the seas and skies of the Northern Hemisphere right up to the Free Mongolian border. Slavia is a spent force in that it had been all but wrecked by three bloody revolutions in 100 years. It had no stomach left for bloodshed.

Ludec no longer has an office routine to stick to but he still feels and acts like a journalist. He takes a hoverer to visit an old friend at Chandler's Ford, near Southampton.

"Sixty mile limit, friend," reminds the driver. "Any more and you'll have to pay."

DM technology may have sent the cost of international travel sky high, but getting around on city streets has never been cheaper.

Ludec resents the threat of having to pay if the meter tips over the limit, but he is heading out of town.

He reaches a sleepy little avenue and walks a few paces to a white garden gate. He stares a moment at the tableau on his friend's front lawn. It is a working model of an ancient watermill, scaled to a fraction of its size. The water bubbles satisfyingly through the blades of the mill, and at a window tiny figurines man a grinding wheel, powered by the flow.

Ludec is always transfixed by this working model which transports him mentally back to the Dark Ages. His friend is a historian and Ludec knows there are many more working models like this one inside the rambling old cottage.

"Prof," he says as he takes a comfortable seat on a floral settee, quietly admiring the darkened oak cross timbers of the ceiling overhead.

"My dear Ludec," says the Prof. "What brings you here to see me in such troubled times?"

"I've lost my job," says Ludec. "At least temporarily, probably permanently."

Professor Harry Guest chuckles into his white beard. "Last thing any of us should be worrying about right now. What happened? Did they get fed up with hearing the truth?"

"Editorial disagreement. Doesn't matter. Anyhow, as far as I know I'm still on full pay, although I don't know for how long."

"So... to what do I owe the pleasure?"

"I want to ask you something. About the ingot."

"We've talked about it before, Ludec. What more could you possibly need to know?"

"Just curious, I suppose. Do you believe the ancients really knew what they had there? Did they somehow... manufacture it? Did they really have the know-how?"

The Prof turns to an antique walnut cabinet and takes a bottle of Scotland's finest single malt. He pours two generous glasses. Nobody has to worry about drink-driving these days.

"As you know, the legend is that it came from Merlin's Cave but no scholar actually believes that," he says, his back still turned to Ludec. "Although that ties in with its estimated age."

"Then who? Who could possibly have harnessed and worked with Dark Matter in the 7th or 8th centuries? It's a field we had only the barest awareness of even in modern times. How could Merlin or anyone else in those days have greater knowledge than ours?"

Even through the straggly wisps of white hair, Ludec can see that the Prof is grinning broadly as he turns to hand him his whisky.

"Who indeed?" The Prof sighs and sits opposite his friend. "There are theories, of course. Visitors from space... an alien intervention. Read the comics. Watch daytime TV."

"There must be an answer," insists Ludec. "Something happened, so what was it?"

"It's not totally unheard of in history," observes the Prof. "We always think of history as some sort of chronological timeline; the invention of fire, the wheel, the steam engine, the combustion engine... "

"But?"

"There are other examples of glitches, although of course not so extreme. We didn't have Moses parting the waves with a nuclear explosion, for instance. Not as far as we can tell, at least." The Professor was smiling, but kindly.

"However, the Babylonians may have experimented with batteries and advanced astronomical lenses long before Christ. There's no absolute proof, but ancient writings suggest a tantalising possibility."

"Yes, I've heard of that sort of thing. Anything else?"

The Prof takes a long, deep draught of his whisky, a glass of pure gold.

"Academically speaking there is no doubt that the progress of civilisation is not the progressive, straight graph we would like it to be," he adds. "That is a myth we cling to because it makes us feel safe. It keeps the Barbarians from the gates, so to speak.

"The truth is that development of growth leaps a few steps and then regresses, forward and then back. In many cases, the actual measurement of civilisation depends on where you are standing in the world at any particular time.

"The Incas in 15th-century South America were straight out of the Dark Ages compared to the Terra-del-Basque conquistadors who appeared on their shores in their fancy, white-sailed galleons firing cannon and musket at their spears and knives.

"Yet the Incas, and even earlier Indian races, had a grasp of irrigation, nursery farming and astronomy far beyond European knowledge. They didn't have the fine castles of the conquistadors, but their temples and palaces stood up to earthquakes some 8.5 on the Richter Scale. They were architectural wonders and yet they were still worshipping the sun and the moon."

Ludec tries to take it all in. "So... the ingot is some kind of 'glitch'?"

"Perhaps. I really don't know. It was made from Dark Matter by someone who knew how to harness and manipulate anti-matter. Who that person was, I have no idea. No one has. But, of course, the real question is: if they knew enough about it to fashion an ingot, why didn't their particular civilisation burgeon and leapfrog centuries?"

Ludec has now developed his own theory. "It all seems to come back to the idea that it was all the work of one man, perhaps a great wizard, who wanted to keep his knowledge a deep secret."

The Prof nods, non-committally. Then they both say it at once: *"Merlin!"*

＊ ＊ ＊ ＊ ＊

His mind is racing as he wanders from the Prof's house to a sorrier side of town. His steps are slow and deliberate, in bloody-minded, contrary contrast to his thoughts. His feet know where they are going, but he hopes his consciousness won't notice.

Ludec knows the street, knows it only too well. The acacia tree in the front garden with the rusty old swing. It has always been rusty, always been old. No child ever comes to sit on that rotten timber seat any more. Yet, when the wind blows high on the darkest night, there may still be the ghost of some child, with the wind blowing in his hair and dreams and plans rushing through his head like a running brook. The hinges will squeak and moan as they may once have done in long-dead days and somebody in the house will turn in their sleep and remember. Just as he is remembering now.

THE EVE OF THE GREAT WAR

He walks on, his steps slow and lumbering, his spirit willing him to stop and turn around. But something else makes him press on, something deep inside. Then he is standing before it. The house. Its garden, in keeping with the rest of the sorry street, is unkempt and unloved. Nothing grows here by design. Everything that flourishes had fought for every inch of sunlight, every drop of rain. Only the ugliest and toughest survived in this wilderness of waste. Yet in this explosion of knotgrass, brambles and chickweed there is still one oasis of foxglove, standing tall and sympathetic against an ancient water butt. Two dragonflies court around its purple flowers, dancing a flittering tango in the rancid air inches from several gallons of green, stagnant waste-water.

Something makes him push the gate wide and urges him to take a step along the path to the door. He stands before the flaking green paint with the wonky Number 22 over the oxidised brass letterbox and surprises himself by shedding a tear. Just one. He wipes it away and stares up at the top right box-room window. He remembers a small boy with his face cupped in his hands, staring out through the small leaded panes and dreaming of... what? Freedom? Escape? Salvation? Love?

His face reveals nothing, but small beads of sweat are gathering on the back of his neck. There is a war being waged within, between heart and brain. He knows not which is on which side. He can feel the urge to stretch out his hand to the gargoyle door-knocker, and he can feel an equal petition not to. The sweat runs cold down his back despite the warmth of the afternoon.

"Ludy? Is that you?" The male voice stumbles clumsily from an upper window, but not the box room. It is a voice he knows and fears. A voice that once made him yearn for his father's cornball jokes and tall stories. He shivers.

He turns sharply around and hurries down the path and out through the gate, hinges squeaking a mild protest. He knows the voice can only be in his head.

"Ludy?"

But he is gone.

LUDEC

* * * * *

Ludec has to order up a hoverer from the city and the two-way journey for the driver pushes him over the pay threshold.

As they drive back, floating across the green hills and farms of Hampshire, the radio is blaring the latest war news.

"Heard the latest?," asks the driver. "Caesaria's joined the war. Hildebrand and Salvatori are marching into Breton right now. Poor buggers don't stand a chance. Edica's ordered our planes in the air. Red, white and blue diagonals all across the clouds. Our West Afrika fleet is sailing to confront the Caesarians in the Med. There'll be a punch-up within days."

Ludec at first curses himself for not keeping abreast of the news while he visited his friend, then relaxes thinking 'what the devil does it matter?' He knew the whole scenario before it happened. It's everyone's problem now. There is something verging on relief that he no longer has to keep up with events for professional reasons.

He decides to call in at The Nugget on the way home and hopes that the editor won't be there. He doesn't want to listen to any more sycophantic apologising from him.

It is getting dark when he pays off the driver and turns towards the door of the pub. What he hasn't noticed until now is that there are a handful of pickets hanging around. They know this is The Trumpet's favourite watering hole. He decides discretion is the better part of valour and heads to the left, away from the entrance. But he is too late – he has already been spotted.

"There's one," shouts a coarse, rough voice.

"That's Strong," yells someone else. "Strong the Sniveller!"

The crowd that approaches him is small but menacing. He stands his ground, facing them.

"Good evening," he says coolly. "Coming in for a drink?"

"What good's all your anti-war propaganda now, Strong? You've been sacked, haven't you? What are you doing here, then? Gonna cry into your beer?"

"Go easy, with him," scoffs another. "His wife is pregnant."

"How'd that happen, then?" quips the first man. "Thought you'd be too busy running away, you yellow-livered scum."

"Not so soft, was he, when he got banged up for butchering that innocent old man?" screams another voice. "Not such a bleeding-heart pacifist then, was he?"

Ludec is so dazed by the mention of his pregnant wife that he hardly feels the first blow. A fist comes at his face from the darkness on his right, away from the lights of the pub. He can feel the broken nose and the taste of blood in his throat.

"Happy now?" he spits through phlegm and bile as he tries to staunch the crimson flow with his bare hands.

"Not quite," says the first man and suddenly he feels half a dozen hands all over him, pulling him bodily towards the alley alongside the Nugget. "Get him down here."

Ludec stumbles forward, unable to resist so many angry arms. In the alley a well-aimed kick to his crotch brings him to his knees and he lies there, among the dustbins and litter. Numb with pain, he turns over on his back and looks up at his tormentors. He can't understand their anger. He is no appeaser, he is just a hack who tried to tell the truth, to warn them.

A pair of hands reaches down to hoist him up by the lapels. He stands there, stupid and shaking, but for just a moment. Then another fist slams into his face, followed by another and then another. Somebody steadies him so he will not fall back to the ground, so he takes blow after blow, mostly to his face and upper body.

Ludec's battered brain spins. He thinks of striking back but it all seems so ridiculous somehow. Here they were, all about to be evaporated by the most lethal weapon ever known to man, and these people want to hurt him. Why? It wasn't him launching the missiles or even leading the government.

But deep inside he knows, and it is this knowledge that stops him raising his fists to retaliate. It is fear. Their fear. His fear. It is all the same. All the same taste.

Finally a series of further kicks to his groin and legs bring him down and his captors give up trying to support him. They let him slump to his smashed knees and his flailing left arm sends a dustbin lid spinning noisily to the ground.

As if at a given signal his attackers disappear soundlessly into the night.

"What's all that noise? Who's chucking dustbin lids around?" Even through his badly bruised senses Ludec is aware that this is Jebbers, the Nugget landlord.

Behind him is a scrum of Ludec's own drinking buddies. "A bit bloody late," Ludec mutters under his breath. He is almost screaming with agony and both his legs feel broken.

"Who's there?" demands Jebbers.

"What is it, Jebs?" another voice that Ludec recognises as Edwin.

"Some hobo, robbed and beaten blind, poor sod," says Jebbers and reaches down to help Ludec to his feet. "Give me a hand here."

"I can't... I can't stand," Ludec manages through a mouthful of broken teeth.

"Jesus, it's Ludec," says Edwin. "Get an ambulance someone. Now!"

* * * * *

Ludec is head to toe in bandages in a private ward at Winchester Camelot Hospital when Alicia rushes in.

"Darling! Luddie, for God's sake," she screams but has to be restrained from getting any closer by a prim nurse in a blue and white uniform.

"He's barely conscious, Mrs Strong," she explains. "He may not be able to respond to you much, if at all. Give him time."

Alicia tears her eyes away from the stranger in the hospital bed to face the nurse.

"Is he... going to be alright?"

"The doctors say there some broken bones and he will be having a scan shortly to discern any brain damage."

Alicia is shocked. "... *some* broken bones? *Brain* damage?"

"Both his legs, I'm afraid, the left fractured in two places. They must have used a weapon of some kind. His skull is badly bruised and scraped but hopefully nothing penetrated. Both arms are badly damaged also."

THE EVE OF THE GREAT WAR

Alicia can't take all this in. "The bloody monsters. Whose side are they on, for God's sake?"

"You can sit with him for a while, if you like, until the scan, but you may not get much out of him. Don't touch him, not even to hold his hand. You understand. Until the doctors have ascertained his precise injuries."

But, no, Alicia does not understand. She turns to the unrecognisable broken body that was once her husband and sits down beside him as the nurse pulls the plastic curtain around them before leaving to attend to more important matters elsewhere.

"Darling," whispers Alicia softly, and remembers just in time not to try and take his hand. "I'm here. It's going to be alright."

But Alicia doesn't think it is going to be alright. She doesn't think anything is going to be alright at all, ever again.

Suddenly she is aware that Ludec is trying to say something. His face is completely bandaged with just a space for his face and mouth. She can't even see his beautiful, blue eyes.

"What is it, darling? I'm here. I'm here." Alicia leans her face closer to hear him better, but takes great care not to brush any part of his smashed body.

"M... m... m...." Ludec is trying desperately to say something.

"What is it, darling. What is it? I'm listening."

"M..m...m..."

"Tell me!"

"Merlin," he says. "It was Merlin."

And behind her tears Alicia knows in advance what the result of the brain scan is going to be.

CHAPTER TWELVE

INTO THE ABYSS

Lily is with her mother in the ward, and smiles for the first time in days when allowed at last to put a comforting hand on her father's brow. He tosses and turns in his own secret, comatose melodrama.

He is barely conscious but the scan fails to show any signs of dangerous concussion or serious damage.

"He's trying to say something again," Lily tells her mother. They both sit anxiously by his bedside, almost around the clock.

"Merlin," he mutters, barely audible. "The Duke chased the fox. The wolf is here."

"He's smiling," says Lily. "He's saying something about a fox and a wolf."

"It was a headline on one of his stories," explains Alicia. "Chase the fox but watch out for the wolf... something like that."

"Daddy, Daddy," urges Lily, but very quietly. Her face is creased in consternation. She has been told not to disturb him unduly. He'll come out of it naturally, the doctor said. Meanwhile he'll drift in and out but it was important not to force him.

Ludec is aware of his daughter's presence. Alicia's too. But he can't respond, even though he wants to.

There's a mist, and a lake. The wolf's tongue is hanging out and he's panting. There are people, but he can't quite make them out. They're friendly, almost intimate somehow. He doesn't know them but they know him. He can feel that. They know him. Suddenly his heart chills as he recognises two figures in the shadows; Marcie and the old man.

Someone is whispering to him: Chase not the fox blindly, lest you find the wolf. Who found the wolf? The wolf is smiling. He isn't hungry.

Hildebrand. The Duke of Normandy.

Hildebrand is spouting on about Aryanism, Nietzsche. She is standing by the lake, watching a straggle of Jews and gypsies shuffle through the mist on the other side. She is holding a gigantic, two-bladed sword, leaning on its hilt, its point downwards in the soft moss.

Ludec is expected to write the leader. The editor is standing at his side, a hand on his shoulder. I need 1,000 words and I need them yesterday.

Ludec's mind stumbles. He looks down at the typewriter keys and they are blank.

Come on, Luddie. Give it to them hard. Tell them what 1,000 years of peace has meant. His fingers are digging into Ludec's flesh.

One thousand words. One word for every year.

Come on, Luddie. You can touch-type, Almost.

Where are the letters?

M. Is this M? M appears on the paper.

Where's E? Is this E? E is there too.

ME.

He tries R. No, that's a T. Backspace. Try again.

On the page, R nestles up to ME.

Now an L... now an I... and an N.

MERLIN.

Merlin steps towards him from the side of the lake, swirling in fog.

Sir Ludec, he says. So you want to be a Knight of the Round Table like Lancelot? Then tell them, tell them what 1,000 years of peace has meant.

Ludec struggles to think. THINK.

Facts.

In Isandlwana, January 1879 Albion Redcoats were wiped out by Zulus who followed up their victory by exterminating a handful of survivors at Rorke's Drift. In Winchester the Albion Republic Government nursed its broken nose and admitted it was an exercise on which they should never have embarked. They never returned. The Zulus prospered in peace and helped forge the Free Afrika we know today.

That's it, screams Kris. Give it to them. Both hands are on Ludec's shoulders now, fingers digging deeper and deeper, and he swears he can feel blood seeping through his shirt.

Facts.

September 1297: William Wallace defeats Longshank's armies at Stirling Bridge. The Albion throne capitulates offering an amnesty which restores all Scotland's rights. Wallace is crowned King of Scotland and by popular demand the capital is renamed Wallaceburn.

That's it, screams Kris.

That's it, encourages Merlin.

The old man, with Marcie on his arm, stares at him accusingly. He can lip-read the word he is mouthing: Pacifist.

Ludec looks down at the keys. All the letters are there now.

He writes:

CHASE NOT THE FOX BLINDLY, FOR THE WOLF IS HUNGRY

Rhineland's swing to the radical right is bringing discordant chaos to the European harmony which has hummed sweetly for centuries. There have been wars, certainly, but they have been localised and generally swiftly concluded. When the dust had settled, there were no great changes on the world map. Some scratches, perhaps, but no scars.

But now Caesaira is also in the throes of a fascist uprising, and the evil Salvatori has used his bullying tactics to seize power in Rome.

Both Rhineland and Caesaira suffered greatly in the pan-European recession, which in turn led to an upsurge in popular support for unpopular politics. The old parties seem tired with nothing new to bring to the table.

Keep it coming, keep it coming, urges Kris.

Poverty remained rife and was a growing problem in both countries. The new Right Wing offers hope and promise; but at a price, a high price.

Caesaira was in steep decline after its glory days of the previous century when Napoleon Bonaparte, born in Corsica under the Caesarian flag, had marched on Rome as a young, renegade soldier-general and united the nation's warring factions.

At last Caesaira was a nation of brothers, sculpted under Napoleon's skilful hands from the rubble of division and disruption.

Napoleon was rightly revered as Caesaira's very own fearless hero, but died from an assassin's bullet in October 1812 at a Napoli Opera House. His body was buried in New Rome on the island of his birth, Corsica.

Ludec pauses. A dichotomy of 1,000 years of peace. Go, go, go, urges Kris, and his fingers continue to dig into the flesh of Ludec's shoulder. We'll make the first edition.

"Mummy," he's mumbling.

"He's dreaming. It'll help his brain to sort itself out before he comes back to us. It's alright."

As 20th century Caesaira went sprinting to the dogs, Albion, with its unique Commonwealth system of trade and commerce which extended to Canada, North America, the Aboriginian continent and Afrika, remained settled and unscathed by the ravages of recession.

It had never had to go to war, apart from a few Indian skirmishes and colonial fighting against the Bretons in Canada, not since the bloody, empire-building campaigns of the Haroldian era 1,000 years before.

Its Pilgrim Fathers had colonised the North Americas and peacefully ceded most of it back to the Americans in the 18th century. Albion kept Canada and was gifted New Winchester and New Winchester state right down to Cape Cod by the Americans as a gesture of gratitude and goodwill.

More, more, screams Kris, desperately checking his watch. He snaps at a copy boy. Get this off to the backbench. Ludec knows the boy. It is Wilson. He caught him smoking in the toilets once. He didn't say anything. Now he watches Wilson running off with the copy, but he's not going to the backbench, he is running to the toilet. Again, Ludec doesn't say anything.

Instead, he writes:

America narrowly averted the tragedy of civil war the following century when the Confederate States abolished slavery overnight, thus forcing Abraham Lincoln to the negotiating table. He had little choice but to broker a peace deal. The nine Confederate states (CSA) lived harmoniously with the United States of North America (USNA) ever since.

A few years earlier the Basque General Santa Anna had appropriated much of the southern slip of the Americas, from Florida to California. He marched north from what used to be Mexico, completely ignoring a fortified mission near Santa Barbara called The Alamo.

He pressed on instead with 7,000 highly trained, crack troops and caught General Sam Houston's infant army napping. Houston was defeated in less than 30 minutes, hacked down in his pyjamas outside the open flap of his tent.

He was found between the bodies of two of his most trusted adjutants. One was 16, the other just turned 15.

Ludec stops for a moment. Think. Facts.

December, 1880: Sheriff Pat Garrett is outgunned by Billy the Kid when a creaking floorboard makes the Kid turn around. Bonney hung up his six-guns and joined a Cowboy Circus. He lived to a ripe old age in peace.

Keep to the point, Luddie.

Albion suffered a bloody 17th century civil war when Oliver Cromwell's New Model Army put an end once and for all to the Divine Right of Kings. Albion had been a proud Republic ever since, despite clinging for nostalgia's sake to such monarchistic anachronisms as Royal Hastings.

Nobody ever cared to challenge that one.

Come on Luddie, we're running out of time. Yes, we are, confirms Ludec. Big time.
Time. Facts.

July 1588: Sir Edrik Dark is playing Fives at Plymouth Hoe when the Terra-del-Basque armada is first spotted in the Channel. "Worry not, lads," he says coolly. "I have a wager on this game. No hurry."

Kris: Luddie... pleeeaaase!

Albion's military might has long been immense, being able to draw on all of its Commonwealth member states (the family). But now the children have begun to bicker. They want grown-up toys of their own and they are prepared to sacrifice centuries of peace for it.

Winchester sanctioned billions upon countless billions of extra revenue for both Caesaira and Rhineland, but burgeoning corruption there meant that it took more than hand-outs to save them from the workhouses of poverty.

The Greater Albion Republic – which incorporates Scotland, Wales, Ireland, Iceland and the entire Scandinavias – has always enjoyed an easy-going detente with Mongolia, whose motives are often obscure but peaceable and non-expansionistic.

Now Chancellor Hildebrand of Rhineland has moved a billion tons of military hardware into Western Slavia, a small Eastern European country nestled right under the wing of the Albion Republic.

Albion is now officially at war with Rhineland and it was no surprise that Caesaira would soon wade in on the fascist side.

One thousand years of peace is slipping into the abyss. Enjoy your breakfast. God help us all.

"He's praying, mummy. Daddy's praying."

CHAPTER THIRTEEN

BATTLE OF ROYAL HASTINGS, 1936

Ludec gazes up at the ceiling, glad to have a quiet moment or two for himself.

Beside his bed, nameless medical accoutrements stand guard like triffids, skeletal cranes of twisted rubber tubing and humming machinery. He has no idea what this equipment is or does. He doesn't want to know. Since he awoke proper, the machines had been wheeled over to his bedside for visits as regular as Alicia's and Lily's. He closes his eyes when this happens, as he tries to close his ears to the ominous bleeps and buzzes of various soft and discreet alarms.

He doesn't want to see the red lights. He fears them almost as much as he fears, at any moment, to hear the sirens.

The doctors will be in soon and, a little after them, his wife and daughter.

His right leg is completely in plaster and a heavy bandage encumbers his left knee. But there is no pain. In fact, everything is numb and this worries Ludec even more. The swelling on his face, especially around his eyes, has gone down considerably and when he had been allowed to look in a mirror he was recognisably Ludec again. Not that he is terribly proud of the face he sees squinting back at him. He is certainly no brave knight on a white charger. He wonders constantly at his apathy when it had come to saving his own skin. He hadn't, he knows, lifted a finger against the thugs who beat him up. It was almost as if he were accepting punishment for a crime of which he felt subconsciously culpable.

BATTLE OF ROYAL HASTINGS, 1936

The soft, soothing music on the radio near his head is suddenly rudely interrupted by a news bulletin. As if by magic, the neat blue and white angel appears out of nowhere and makes to switch the set off. Ludec feels that this is even ruder than the news update.

"Please... please leave it," mumbles Ludec, barely coherent.

"We don't want you getting stressed, Mr Strong. Are you quite sure?" She tilts her face like a bird to catch the subtlest nuance of uncertainty.

"I want to hear."

She hesitates a moment, her finger still hovering over the button, then she changes her mind and makes a show of tucking him in instead.

"We're all moving into a special safe basement, very soon," she tells him, but her eyes are averted. She is keeping secrets, he thinks.

"We'll keep disruption to a bare minimum and we'll all be as comfortable there as we are here."

Ludec thinks of telling her that he doesn't feel particularly comfortable here either, but restrains himself.

"Thank you," he manages.

The blue and white angel exits stage right, under a sign that says QUIET PLEASE. He knows that in a little room just beyond the sign she sits and drinks tea and reads her book, quietly. He knows this because she tells him. She also tells him about her boyfriend who says it will all be over in a few days and that there is absolutely nothing to worry about. Once Hildebrand realises Albion will not just lay still while she brings bedlam to a sleepy Europe.

QUIET PLEASE.

When she realised who he was, the nurse also told him that she had seen his name in the Trumpet. If she knew that this was the very reason he had received his injuries she didn't say so.

The radio brings him back to the real world.

... Salvatori's Caesairian troops are joining the Rhinelanders in a joint pincer movement threatening to crush defenceless Breton. As the tanks of the fascist axis rumble unchecked across Breton's crumbling Maginot Line, President LeSavier this morning called a hasty war cabinet in the capital Lyons.

"We are lost,' he told them earlier today. He added: "Unless Albion can stop the fascists, we are lost. It is imperative we defend our northern beaches to allow the Albions to launch a counter offensive."

But in Breton this is not a popular plan. We have in the studio Sir Michael Mount, Albion's Minister of Defence. "Sir Michael... what do you see happening in Lyons?"

"The Bretons are a small but proud nation, anxious to keep themselves apart from their neighbours, including Albion across the Channel. They have always resented any intrusion by foreign politics. They are sandwiched between the massive Terra-del-Basque and Rhineland. Yet I fear this plan will be hotly debated."

"If I may interrupt you, Sir Michael. We have just heard that Bouvier, a veteran of the controversial Algerian campaigns has told the cabinet, and I quote: 'It would be like an invasion on two sides. I implore the president to allow us to fight the fascists on our own.'"

"Unfortunately," Sir Michael butts in on the news presenter. "they haven't a prayer on their own. There's no love lost with Terra-del-Basque who regard both Albion and Breton as Godless infidels and they won't allow us to land anywhere along their coast. They will remain staunchly neutral. Our only option – Breton's only option – is to allow us to land our forces on the tiny stretch of Breton available to us."

* * * * *

Meanwhile in Lyons, LeSavier's plan to protect the northern beach for the Albions finally gets the reluctant go-ahead after hours of fierce debate.

He petulantly and noisily gathers together all his documents on the assembly hall podium and mutters almost to himself: "They'd have come anyway – with or without an invitation. Thank God."

Literally within minutes of the decision Albion's mighty navy is deployed off the Channel, ready to sail for the slim, pitiful sliver of Breton coast open to them, an area stretching east of Calais.

BATTLE OF ROYAL HASTINGS, 1936

Earlier, a much smaller fleet of three aircraft carriers and 24 destroyers set sail from Albion's protectorates on the west coast of Free Afrika, its brief to police Caesairia's southern flank from the Mediterranean. In turn, the Caesarian navy, not as formidable but significant all the same, is steaming west through the Mediterranean to prevent them getting any closer.

Eighteen hours after the Lyons decision, the Albion fleet encounters the Caesarian ships just off Alexandria and after a deafening action lasting just three-quarters of an hour, ploughs on through the warm, now unprotected seas towards Sicily.

In their wake they have left devastation. Almost the entire Caesarian navy is wrecked at the bottom of the ocean, or listing uselessly in circles. Six Albion ships are also sunk, and one aircraft carrier too badly damaged to continue.

Under the Rules of Engagement she is allowed to pull into Alexandria to effect repairs and finds herself in the neutral port with two Caesarian frigates, holed just above the water line. Absurdly, the aircraft carrier's Captain Ansel Jacobsen finds himself invited for cocktails aboard one of the two frigates. He declines, but politely.

"I find myself unable to avail myself of your hospitality and the undoubted pleasures of your fine Caesairian wines on account of a certain, unfortunate misunderstanding between your President and ours. I feel sure that sanity shall prevail very soon and then I should be delighted to join you on your illustrious destroyer."

"If it doesn't sink first," jokes his number two as he is shown the RSVP, his captain is about to return.

* * * * *

Ludec is sitting up in bed, his pillows dutifully puffed by his eager blue and white angel. He is still listening gravely to the news broadcasts.

He has heard that Albion's bombers are pounding the encroaching axis lines which have finally merged in central Breton. Lyons itself is under siege. Fighters strafe the lines of munitions and military hardware, now spreading its bullying weight across the entire length and breadth of tiny Breton. But no matter how hard the enemy lines are hammered, the joint Caesarian and Rhineland forces seem unstoppable. Ludec bites his lower lip and wonders where Alicia and Lily are at this very moment. But then:

> *...this just in. Albion's Mediterranean fleet has reached the tip of Sicily and we have heard, can this be right, Sir Michael? We have heard... yes... it is confirmed.... Naples has surrendered without a fight."*

Sir Michael is adjusting his own earphones which are keeping him informed of events outside the studio.

> *"It is confirmed... not a single gun has been fired,"* Sir Michael says. *"This is a huge breakthrough and may well prove very significant indeed. Salvatori has crumbled even before the match and it remains to be seen what will happen in Breton over the next few hours. I can't see any other recourse for him other than to withdraw his troops. Pull them right out. Hildebrand is not going to be at all pleased by this... "*

Ludec looks up as Alicia and Lily come into the ward. They are clearly pleased to see him sitting up.

"Are you supposed to be listening to this?" Alicia asks, concerned. "It's a little... distressing for you."

"Distressing it's not," he replies. "Caesairia has collapsed. This will help the fight to save Breton."

Lily clasps her hands together in glee. "Does this mean it's all over? There'll be no bombs?"

Alicia puts her arm around her as she anticipates the gravity of Ludec's reply.

"Nobody can promise that yet, I'm afraid. But things are not quite as glum as they were yesterday. I still want you to go to the US," he throws Alicia a beseeching look, which she ignores.

"We've been told by matron we can stay with you in the basement after today," she says. "Built like a bunker down there, apparently," she adds excitedly, mainly for Lily's benefit.

"What's a bunker?" Lily replies, mystified.

*　*　*　*　*

Within two hours Salvatori has recalled his troops from Breton and Rhinelanders are shocked to find themselves ordered to shoot their retreating, erstwhile comrades.

In confusion the advance stutters and grinds to a halt. Lyons rejoices. The dogs at the gates have stopped barking. For the moment.

In the Albion Channel, the main Albion fleet sails from south-coast bases at Plymouth, Southampton, Portsmouth and Royal Hastings.

"Now we're in for some action," whispers naval rating Sonny West to his comrade as together they pull in the gang-plank. "Hildebrand will wish she never tried to mess with us."

Sonny knows their plan is an amphibious landing on the Breton coast where, protected by heavy naval guns, infantry troops and heavy hardware including tanks, artillery and jeeps will swoop down to free the besieged Bretons. He won't be going ashore, and for that he is sorry. His job will be to remain on his ship not only to protect and guard the beachhead, but to cover the retreat, if needed, when it is all over. A true patriot, Sonny has no doubt that the Albion Expeditionary Force will be entirely successful.

"Those Rhinelanders don't stand a chance," he tells his mate as they work, watching the shores of his homeland recede behind them. "We'll be home again in no time – heroes. Think of the kudos of that, Wilf." He nudges his partner in the lower ribs with a wink. "Won't have to buy a pint for a year. Keep your albis in your pocket."

"That's not all you'll have to keep in your pocket," grins Wilf. "Girls flock to heroes."

"Everyone likes heroes. Especially handsome ones like you and me. Let's get at 'em." Wilf isn't sure whether he means get at the Rhinelanders or the girls, but he smiles anyway and they divide to carry on with their separate duties elsewhere on the busy, noisy desk. Whistles are blowing, commands shouted and even now the cheering from the harbourside departure still rings in their ears.

"Get a move on, lad," sparks Victory's First Officer Daniel Clark as Sonny nearly trips over his shiny, black shoes.

"Sorry, sir."

Daniel watches Sonny go as he makes sharply for the ladder rungs to disappear out of sight over the top.

Then Daniel too withdraws from the bustling deck and returns to the bridge.

"All correct?" asks Admiral Stuart Mackintosh, his immaculately laundered white suit almost literally reflecting his enormous pride at being at the helm of the fleet's flagship, The Victory.

Every Albion flagship has been thus called since Hadrian Neillsen's 144-gun vessel defeated a combined and superior force of Bretons and Basques at the Battle of Biscay in 1805. Lord Neillsen, the son of a Norfolk clergyman, won the day with inspired and revolutionary naval tactics and was hailed a national hero, despite being prone to sea-sickness. Towards the end of the battle, a Breton sniper firing from deck to deck took out Neillsen's one good eye and he spent the rest of his life totally blind under the loving care of his loyal mistress Lady Hamilton at Merton and later in Naples.

She famously said: "He may see no ships but he has only to look into his heart to see me."

Around the latest Victory, now in light seas, all 300 destroyers, frigates, aircraft carriers and troop carriers are Admiral Mackintosh's to command. One word from his lips and they will sail full steam to hell itself. And perhaps they will, he thinks. Perhaps they will.

"All correct," confirms Daniel. "The men are raring to go. Eager for a fight."

"Then we mustn't disappoint them," mutters the Admiral sternly, his naval binoculars trained on the swell before his bow. He knows that before they reach the Breton coast they are going to have to contend with the Rhineland fleet, pressing forward to cut them off in the Channel at this very moment.

Theirs is a fleet of equal size and power. The Admiral doesn't know how events will unfold over the next few hours, but he knows it is likely to be bloody exciting. Rarely had the Albion fleet ever been involved in hostile engagement. The few times they had seen action it had been more like police work. Gunboat diplomacy. This was a full-scale invasion force. Unfortunately, so was the enemy's.

* * * * *

Ludec is telling Lily a story. She is perched on the side of his hospital bed. Alicia is content to sit in the corner behind her, half listening, half reading a magazine.

"Sir Lancelot could not let the damsel suffer like that, tied to a tree with the flames of the dragon's breath flaring just inches away... "

"What did he do? Did he draw his sword?"

"Strangely, Sir Lancelot did NOT draw his sword... " and then, because Lily looks disappointed, quickly adds: "but from his saddle-bag he pulled something even stranger... something even the biggest, fiercest dragon on earth could not defeat."

"What is it? What is it? A gun? A super-dooper gun?"

"They didn't have guns in those days," Ludec admonishes her with a look. "You know that. No, this was something far more dangerous – Merlin's Ingot!"

"The Inglynut," shouts Lily excited, and her mother puts her finger to her lips and points to the sign, QUIET PLEASE. Lily doesn't turn around so she doesn't see.

"The ingot," confirms Ludec. "Just as it looks as if nothing can save the damsel fair from the evil creature's breath of flame, he holds it out in the palm of his hand... "

"Hooray," says Lily, but quieter this time. "Does the dragon die?"

Ludec pauses for dramatic effect. "The dragon sees the ingot in Sir Lancelot's hand and at first seems to sneer at it and him. The lady is struggling with the ropes around her waist and is trembling. Then it happens... "

"What happens?"

"The dragon, having never seen an ingot before, believes it is just more treasure and secretly thinks it would look grand sitting on the top of his pile of glittering jewels in his cave. So he sniffs at the knight's hand, and then... out pops his tongue and he swallows the ingot whole!"

"Yuck," says Lily. "He'll have to get it back later from his dragon doo-doos. Double yuck!"

"But... " Ludec goes on. "Just as the dragon again turns his attention to the girl, his eyes suddenly go all funny and the fire stops shooting out of his mouth. He starts to cough and choke and his vision clouds over... "

"Hooray. Hooray," shouts Lily. Shush, urges her mother behind her, smiling.

"The dragon does a sort of flip over on his back and lies there, dead. Sir Lancelot triumphantly steps forward and places a victorious foot on the dragon's belly, turning to smile at a very relieved damsel not now in distress."

"Yuck. But that means Sir Lancelot will have to dig around in his belly for the ingot. You can't have a knight of the Round Table doing that. His sword will get all messy with dragon's doo-doo."

"Just then... " Ludec continues, raising his finger and pointing it in the air. "The nasty dragon gave a last splutter and, whoosh, out pops the ingot which lands precisely at the damsel's feet. Sir Lancelot pockets it and then rescues her from her bondage."

"Does he kiss her?"

"Good lord, no. Sir Lancelot would never have taken advantage of a lady in distress."

"Hardly worth being rescued, then," whispers Alicia from behind, still thumbing the pages of her magazine.

"You would have kissed her, wouldn't you daddy? If it had been mummy tied to the tree and you had rescued her."

Ludec shoots Alicia a sly glance. "Providing we had been properly introduced first, of course."

"Oh daddy, you really ARE Sir Ludec," says Lily, forgetting for a moment he is still a patient and throwing her arms carelessly around his neck. "You would be brave and save mummy from the fierce dragon. I know you would."

Ludec can suddenly feel all the pain in his limbs return; the fractures, the bruises, the scars. They make him visibly wince, to remind him of what he inescapably sees as his lack of valour.

Alicia can see where all this is leading and hastily puts down the magazine to rise from her seat to go to him.

"Of course he would."

"No, I don't think so," he says sadly. "No shining knight. And no white charger, either."

* * * * *

The two fleets confront each other mid-ocean at a point level with the Albion port of Royal Hastings. A strange silence fills the afternoon as 600 mighty ships stand and stare at each other, ever watchful.

"Jesus, will you look at that." Sonny breathes to his shipmate Wilf. He is ashamed to find that he is quaking, just a little.

"A bloodbath. It's going to be a bloody bloodbath," adds Wilf, whistling through his blackened teeth.

Sonny surveys the massed ranks of their own high-flying flags, the sea, choppier now, the only demarcation between them and the unbroken field of Rhineland insignia.

"The red, white and blue diagonals meet the black fascist flashes," muses Sonny. Almost the only sound is that of the waves lapping all around them. Everything, even the seagulls, seem to be posing the question: What happens next?

Things are more frenzied on the bridge of the flagship Victory. Daniel has ordered, because HE has been ordered to do so, a hurried message to obtain up-to-date orders from High Command in Winchester. This was a development all had anticipated, yet oddly nobody had actually formulated a plan. The consequences were just too horrific to contemplate. It was the ostrich with his head in the sand syndrome.

So far, not a single shot had been fired. What everybody needed to know was 'when would the slaughter begin?'

"High Command is leaving it all up to the officer in the field. Their words," says Daniel as he hands the Admiral the message that has been handed to him by an orderly from the radio room.

"Yes, I suppose that's me," sighs the Admiral, known as 'Cap'n Blue' because of the piercing hue of his penetrating eyes.

"And what the fuck am I going to do? We press the button and we all go up. If we don't, we all go up anyway."

"Tough one," ventures Daniel staring ahead at the line of floating death machines blocking their course. More than 300 ships armed to the teeth with nuclear armaments and undoubtedly Dark Matter bombs too, floating as serenely as ducks in a pond.

"Never thought I'd say it, but I'm glad you're the boss."

* * * * *

Alicia is very much afraid Ludec is going to cry, despite the presence of Lily. It is something he would never have done before, but this is a different Ludec laying there in the hospital bed. An unhorsed, defeated knight.

Lily gets up to allow her mother to take her place. She too realises something is wrong. Alicia takes Ludec's hand in hers.

"You have done everything in your power to fight for good, Luddie. You campaigned fearlessly in the paper despite the hostility it was bound to generate. You must have known it could cost you your job yet you persevered. You didn't flinch. You did what you knew was right."

He smiles at her, with sad, watery eyes, unconvinced eyes.

"I let those thugs smash me to pieces. I didn't lift a finger. It was almost as if I wanted them to beat me up."

"Luddie, it wasn't the least bit like that. I know that if it had been my safety or Lily's at stake, you would have fought like a lion. I know you would, I know you. But in some strange way you felt, wrongly, that this was perhaps your fate – because you believed you had failed. Nobody listened to you and so we are at war. They took their fear out on you and you let them; you consciously let them. You knew it wasn't you they were screaming at, it was something else. Believe me, you were a knight to the last and we're proud of you."

"THEY weren't very proud of me, were they, that lot outside The Nugget?"

"Luddie, you're always going on about being distantly related to Sir Ludec and now you think you are a disgrace to his memory. But you really are no different from him, not in any sense.

BATTLE OF ROYAL HASTINGS, 1936

"Didn't you tell me that he too faced ridicule and scorn because he advised the King to wait before rushing into battle with the Norman duke? Well, what if – when he finally went to the King and gave him this unpopular advice – they had ripped him apart like feeding lions? Do you think Sir Ludec would have fought back? Do you really think he would have fought before the King to save his skin? I believe he would have done exactly what you did – nothing! He would have accepted his fate, just as you did. Those people at The Nugget were not your enemies – you knew that and so you couldn't fight them. Sir Ludec would have felt exactly the same if they had butchered him like those thugs almost butchered you."

Lily had gone around to the other side of her father's bed. She didn't really understand what was wrong, but she knew he was upset and that her mother was trying to comfort him.

"I think you really are a shining knight on a white charger, daddy," she sobs. "And you don't need the inglynut, you are already a hero."

Ludec isn't in pain any more. He's stopped hurting – inside and out.

"Thank you, ladies," he says. "Let's just hope some other knight can get us out of this war before we all go up in smoke. I've hung up my sword."

* * * * *

On the bridge of the Victory all eyes are still glued to binoculars, trained on the ominous presence of the enemy fleet.

"One thing's for sure, they aren't going to wave us through," says the Admiral in a way that shows his First Officer that he has made a decision.

"Tell all ships to file dead ahead: every ship to pick its own course through the enemy and at the first sign of any trouble, fire at will. But not to wait before they're sunk before responding."

"Operational level, sir?" requests Daniel, and the Admiral pauses for just a moment.

"All levels," he replies. "All damned levels, as required."

Daniel turns to the radio room orderly who has written everything down. He nods and the two men share a glance that says: this is it.

They both know 'all levels' means conventional, atomic and DM. The First World War is indeed going to be the Last World War. From here on in, it'll be back to sticks and stones, if there's anyone around still strong enough to throw them.

The orderly hurries to the radio room and Daniel feels his pulse starting to race.

"Half ahead," commands the Admiral and Daniel communicates the order to the engine room. Within seconds the ship throbs once again with the surging power that thrills every sailor. They once again hold dominion over the ocean, not just sitting still like bobbing corks completely at its mercy.

Daniel can feel the forward movement and wonders how long any of them have to live. Perhaps minutes, perhaps only seconds. But he knows they are doing the only thing possible in the circumstances. He watches their bow making steadily, defiantly for the Rhineland line.

The waves part almost respectively. We who are about to die, salute you, thinks Daniel.

"Sir! Sir!" It is the radio room orderly. His eyes are both nervous and excited as he rushes onto the bridge to hand Daniel a sheet of paper. Daniel glances at it but knows there is no time to spare, and hands it straight to the Admiral.

"All stop," he says softly and Daniel immediately passes the order on to the chief engineer in the engine room. Then he stares at the Admiral, his eyes demanding to hear the latest news.

"This is a communiqué from the Rhineland naval Admiral Otto von Bersch. It is addressed to me by name," says the Admiral slowly.

"It says: 'The Mongolian High Command insists that we return to Rhineland ports, immediately and with haste. Our troops in Breton and Western Slavia are also to lay down their arms and withdraw from battle.'"

The radio room orderly is back again with another message which is handed to the Admiral through the First Officer.

"What the hell is going on?" says Daniel, baffled.

"We have here more or less the same communiqué," says the Admiral, reading the sheet of paper in his hands. "The Mongolians have very kindly offered not to deploy two dozen nuclear and DM submarines hidden at present in the depths of the Caspian and Black Seas to annihilate every city in Rhineland if Hildebrand complies immediately."

The First Officer smiles grimly as he puts the glasses back to his eyes. He can feel the palpable tension in the entire fleet as he scours the enemy force, from one ship to the next.

"Let's hope that this invitation comes with an immediate RSVP," he says.

They are just a few miles off the coast from Royal Hastings, face-to-face with the massive Rhineland fleet and counting down to a naval action that will wreak Armageddon upon the entire world.

Then two things happen at once. The already taut muscles of Daniel's heart physically spasm as Albion foghorns mysteriously begin to blast; first one, then a second and then a third. Only now does he see it himself. One of the Rhineland destroyers starts to steam in a gentle arc, slowly turning away to the east, followed by another and then another.

Now there is a cacophonous roar of foghorns as the Albion fleet noisily salutes the withdrawing Rhineland fleet, cowed into submission by the weight of the persuasive Mongolian argument. It is so loud it can be heard miles away on the Sussex coast where people rejoice because they somehow sense what it suggests even before they hear it on the news.

"I suppose this means we can go home?" says the First Officer, his glasses still firmly trained on the retreating ships, his grin as wide as the ocean.

The Admiral is steely-eyed, inscrutable. Almost impassively he watches the huge exodus melt away before him. The Kraken is awake; the sleeping giant has stirred and the world, with good cause, trembles.

"Yes, stand down, Number One. For Now.

"Write this up as another date for the history books: The Battle of Royal Hastings, 1936. A victory for common sense."

-Ends-

EPILOGUE

Hospitals aren't where you'd usually expect people to let their hair down, but fiesta fever has come to the Winchester Camelot. The wards are festooned with coloured balloons and flags, and even the blue and white angel moves from bed to bed with an extra chirpiness.

With much relief the bunker basement has been decommissioned without a single customer. Ludec is sitting up in bed with Alicia and Lily at his side. Alicia has given him a newspaper, The Illustrated London News, a national daily published in Albion's second city.

The headline indignantly roars:

PEACE HERO SACKED AND BEATEN FOR SPEAKING OUT

"There's a picture of you the day they brought you to hospital, daddy. Don't look at it," Lily tries, in vain, to cover the horrific shot of blood, twisted limbs and bruises with her arm. But Ludec has already seen it. Jebbers and Edwin trying desperately to help the stretcher fight through a small crowd on the street outside. He was touched they had both come with him to the hospital.

"No war so everyone's hungry for something else to fill the front pages," says Ludec, wearied, and dismissively shoves the paper away from his lap.

Alicia takes it and carefully folds it before putting it back in her bag.

"They've been on the TT. It hasn't stopped ringing. They are disgusted with what's happened to you. They want to offer you a job. In fact, everybody does."

With what seems an enormous effort, Ludec smiles. Kris has already been in to visit and to offer him his old job back.

EPILOGUE

"It was only while feelings were running so high," he had said, that nervous smile that Ludec hates so much playing on his lips like it was afraid of either dropping to the floor or being swallowed whole.

Ludec had told him he'd think about it, but privately believed it was high time to move on. He had plenty of options, including TV stations in the USNA.

"Prentice sends his best regards. He is very concerned for you," was Kris's parting shot.

I bet, thought Ludec.

Through heavy eyes he looks at Lily who is as usual perched anxiously at his bedside. Alicia is in her usual chair behind.

"The war's all over, daddy! Was it because of your campaign?"

"No, darling. Not really."

"But you had to do it? Just like Sir Ludec would have. Was Hildebrand the dragon?"

"Yes, she was."

"And she swallowed the inglynut because she's stupid. Is she dead now?"

"No, not dead. But she learned a powerful lesson."

She cocks her head to one side quizzically, prompting Ludec to reply.

"Détente."

"Daytant? What's daytant?"

"If your neighbour has as big a stick as yours it's not wise to go and steal his sugar."

"So she'll steal it from someone else with a smaller stick."

"That's where it gets complicated."

Alicia leans forward, a worried expression on her face.

"I think we should let daddy sleep now so he can get fit and well all the sooner."

They notice that he has succumbed quietly but suddenly to sleep and both rise to kiss him gently on the lips, careful not to awaken him.

He is off the critical list, the doctors have said, but he still has some way to go before recovery. He's not out of the woods yet. Something in his mental state is still worrying them, but they hope the secret mechanics of his mind will sort it out naturally.

LUDEC

Light of heart and with hope, Alicia and Lily depart leaving Ludec alone with his dreams.

* * * * *

He's back at the house at Chandler's Ford, standing before the wonky 22 and gargoyle door-knocker. He knocks and there are footsteps inside. The door creaks open.

"I knew you'd come," it's that impossible male voice.

He steps in and follows the shuffling old man through to an old-fashioned, musty parlour.

"How've you been, Ludy?" The old man is settling into a flower-print sofa, gesturing for Ludec to sit down beside him. Ludec takes an armchair opposite. It's dusty but has the advantage of distance.

"You came before, didn't you? More than once."

"More than once," Ludec agrees, his fingers intertwined before him, agitated.

"Why didn't you stop and talk? Why did you run?"

"Talk about what?"

"You're here now. Do you plan to sit there silent as a mouse?"

Ludec is silent as a mouse.

"I didn't force anybody to bring you here, you know. I didn't get down on my knees and beg your father to let me look after you for a while."

"Dad was – busy," murmurs Ludec in reply.

"Yes. Just for a while."

Somewhere deep in his consciousness Ludec can hear a bleep. Just one.

The old man shuffles in his seat. "I know you weren't happy here. I tried my best, you know."

Ludec raises his eyes to his and stops interlacing his fingers. He puts his hands in his pockets and has to lean forward a little to do so. His hands are safer there. The old man is safer with them there.

"You used to tell me my father didn't want me."

"I never said that. Perhaps... when you made me angry... "

"A 12-year-old boy made you angry?"

EPILOGUE

"You were a tough little lad. You knew your own mind. When Marcie was alive she used to say 'he's as stubborn as a mule'. Remember that?"

Ludec lowers his gaze. He doesn't remember. He doesn't want to remember. There are too many other things...

"She bought you books, history books. I've still got a stack of 'em here somewhere. Dark Ages stuff. You were all wrapped up in ancient history."

"You said I was obsessed."

"It's not good to be quite so single minded. The past is dead, we move on."

"You said I was completely bats," Ludec is raising his voice now. "You said I was touched with Merlin-madness and should wake up to the real world. You said... "

The old man interrupted him with a raised hand. "I said no such thing. I just tried to get you interested in other things. Sport, art, literature... "

"You locked them away, my books."

"I had to keep the house tidy. They were everywhere. It's just a small house."

"When that didn't work you locked *me* away."

"You... became intolerable. I had to tell your father."

"No, you said you were going to tell my father but you didn't, did you? You didn't tell him anything. You were more than happy to have a little boy around to be cruel to. Locking me up in my room, robbing me of my books. You only let me out if Marcie noticed something."

"You were obsessed, Ludy. Bloody obsessed. You thought you *were* Sir Ludec straight out of the pages of history. You talked as if you personally knew him. It was insane."

"Is that why you made up that story? Is that why you told Marcie I came at you with a kitchen knife, deliberately scratching yourself with it to draw a little blood?"

The old man began tut-tutting under his wheezy breath. "I'm afraid your memory is a little clouded, Ludy. The sad truth is you did come at me with the knife and that's when Marcie and I decided to tell your father we couldn't look after you any more. But we never told him the truth."

"The truth?" Ludec is shouting now, his face an angry shade of red. Somewhere his senses detect a red light, flashing intermittently and a low buzzing noise.

"The truth is you took great pleasure in locking me away all night and most of the day, telling Marcie I just wanted to be alone to read. But I had nothing to read, did I? You took away everything and just let me sob. Marcie let me be because she saw me as your responsibility, dad's friend. Dad's *good* friend."

"Your memory is really a little distorted. You should calm down. I did my very best for you."

"Including those things you liked to do to me before you allowed me any supper... were they 'best for me' too?"

Ludec has leapt to his feet and is screaming now over a frenzy of flashing lights and urgent, metronomic bleeps. Despite the mayhem, he can still hear Marcie's long, piercing scream. The knife plunges, again and again. His stomach churns as he watches the face below him dissolve to a twisted palate of scarlet and corpse grey.

Even now the old man's lips are moving in their deathly pallor and he delivers a final accusation with his last gasping breath:

"YOU HAD YOUR REVENGE, DIDN'T YOU? LUDEC THE FUCKING PACIFIST HAD HIS REVENGE."

* * * * *

While the rest of the world celebrates its rescue from the edge of the abyss, Ludec's attendant machinery bursts into mournful song.

Desperate buzzes and blips from medical paraphernalia at his bedside immediately conjures a rush of doctors and nurses who wheel him without hesitation into intensive care.

But no shocks, paddles or ECGs are enough to coax his tired and battered soul back to the world of the living.

He flat-lines.

The medical staff sadly but resignedly remove their masks and press the final red button. All is suddenly silent.

EPILOGUE

"Please record TOD at 4.00am nurse," whispers the doctor, wiping the back of his hand over his perspiring forehead.

None of them notice two oddly dressed spectral figures standing hand in hand beside Ludec's body.

One looks up at her husband's face for permission and when, with a solemn smile, he nods, she places a strikingly patterned kerchief on the pillow beside Ludec's head.

Even the blue and white angel doesn't see it as she pulls the sheet all the way up over his body.

The next morning attendant medical staff, mildly mystified, discard the scarf in a bin marked 'Non-Contagious Only' and so Alicia never learns of its existence.

But in his last moment of earthly consciousness, Ludec knew full well its significance and took his leave with a strangely serene smile.

-Endswww.eleusinianpress.co.uk